4th of July
in
Sweetwater County

Book VII
Sweetwater County
Series

Ciara Knight

Also by Ciara Knight

Sweetwater County
Winter
Spring
Summer
Fall
Christmas
Valentines Day
Thanksgiving

The Neumarian Chronicles
Weighted
Escapement
Pendulum
Balance

Battle For Souls
Rise From Darkness
Fall From Grace
Ascension of Evil

The Shrouded Kingdoms
The Curse of Gremdon
The Secrets of Dargon
The Runes of Bramon

A Prospector's Novel
Fools Rush

www.ciaraknight.com

4th of July in Sweetwater County – Sweetwater County Series
Ciara Knight
ISBN-13: 978-1-939081-27-8

This novel would not be possible without the endless dedication of so many. A special thank you to: my family for all their love and support, my editor Cora Artz, my cover artist Robin Ludwig, and my amazing street team members.

CHAPTER ONE

Seated in her parked Oldsmobile, Julia Cramer watched the shop owners of Creekside bustle about opening their stores, all of them oblivious of her crumbling son. Loss had broken him. Even now, a year after his father's death, he struggled.

"Don't leave me, Mommy." Ryan's bottom lip puckered and early morning light sparkled off his tear-streaked face.

Julia gripped the steering wheel, despite the fact she'd already dropped the keys into her purse. *God, why'd you have to take Henry from us?*

People walked along Main Street, some waved, others nodded.

Julia forced a smile in return then managed the courage to glance at her son's small frame. A mini-version of his dad, Ryan had the same dark wavy hair, big brown eyes, and full binary attitude. Everything was right and wrong, black and white in the world.

He swiped a knuckle across his nose and straightened his shoulders. "I don't want to stay with no one else. I want to be home with you."

"I'm sorry, honey, but I need to finish my degree if

I'm going to get a better job."

Ryan fisted his tiny hands and hammered his thighs. "I don't care about money." He threw the car door open and fled, running down the sidewalk, dodging other pedestrians. Passing the pink and purple bouquets in front of the flower shop, and the display of Victorian furniture in the front bay window of J and L Antiques, he finally halted outside the large picture windows of Café Bliss.

The summer heat trapped inside her beater Oldsmobile suffocated her with hot air and loneliness. *If only*, she thought, those two words running on an endless loop for the last year. If only Henry hadn't died, their life would be so different.

Julia snagged her purse and shoved the door open with a loud, rusty creak. She slammed the door and stepped onto the sidewalk, but Ryan had already bolted inside Café Bliss.

Miniature American flags set out to celebrate the country's independence, flapped with the promise of a coming summer storm. Most people thought of July 4th as an excuse to have a barbeque and light fireworks, forgetting that it was really a celebration of freedom. Freedom that had cost Henry his life.

Sheriff Mason held the door to Café Bliss open for her. "Good morning."

"Good morning," she replied.

He tipped his hat in that southern gentleman way. "Trianna wanted to find out if you and Ryan were going to be at the 4th of July celebration this year." While his tone was light and cheerful, she could still hear the underlying pity.

Keeping her eyes fixed on the door handle, she said, "I don't know yet."

Before the sheriff could reply, his radio blared. "Sorry. I've got to run. Hope we see you there."

She nodded vaguely then stepped into Café Bliss. The smell of fresh brewed coffee and the sound of espresso machines working overtime filled the air. Cathy West joined her at the door, a bag in hand that promised extra sewing work tonight. Thank goodness Julia's grandmother had taught her to sew. If not, she wouldn't have been able to work at night for Cathy. And that extra money came in handy.

"What's wrong with Ryan? I thought he was gonna knock me over with the force of a bull charging a clown in the rodeo."

Julia couldn't help but snicker at Cathy's colorful speech. "He's upset."

"What's he upset about?" Cathy asked.

Julia sighed. "I won't be home again tonight. I've got an interview over at Riverbend for the nursing program."

Cathy eyed Ryan huddled on a chair, his knees drawn to his chest. "Why does that upset him? You're trying to make a better life for you both. That's a good thing, darling."

The bell above the door jingled and a group of teens, wearing cutoffs and bathing suits, entered the café, most likely on their way to the lake. Julia watched them sashay up to the counter, trying to ignore the twinge of envy at their carefree attitudes. "He doesn't like me being away so much, but it will definitely bring more money in. Then we can have more time together, without me having to work two jobs."

"Speaking of two jobs, you sure you want all this?" Cathy held out the bag of sewing projects.

Julia nodded with as much enthusiasm as she could manage. It wasn't a matter of want, it was a must if she was going to stay out of debt.

Cathy handed her the bag. "All right then. Directions are inside. I can get them from you tomorrow or the next day." Turning, she joined Judy Benjamin at a table near the register.

For a moment, Julia watched them sip their lattes and chitchat, the ugly monster of jealousy nipping the back of her neck. Why'd Judy get her happily-ever-after? James, the love of her life had returned from war forty years after being declared dead. Yet there was no such chance for Henry. It didn't matter how long she waited. He was never coming home. He wasn't missing in action as James had been. He was dead, killed senselessly by friendly fire.

Ryan sat at the side counter, staring out the large windows at the mountains. That all too familiar shot of anger on his face pierced her heart with sniper accuracy.

She swallowed the lump of mourning, fostered her veteran widow duty, and joined him. "I'm sorry. I wish there was another way," she said, snuggling Ryan into her side.

"I don't want to stay with Mrs. Fletcher. She always talks about her dead husband." Ryan inhaled a ragged breath, a bandage breath to cover the wound of no father. "Why can't I go with you? I'll be good, I promise. I can sit quietly and read."

She pressed a kiss to his forehead and inhaled the musky scent of his big-boy shampoo. He was growing up so fast. He deserved to play with friends and have a life beyond her burdens. "I know you'd be good. It's not that. Please, will you give it a try? We need this. If I'm able to get a job in nursing I won't have to work seventy hours a week at two jobs to pay the bills." Ryan sighed and she continued, "That'll mean more time for us to play Clash of Clans on our iPads together."

He smiled, a marathon-video-game-with-cookies smile. "I'll try," he muttered.

Julia messed his hair. "Thanks, buddy."

Mrs. Fletcher sauntered like Grace Kelly toward them with a cup in each hand. "Here you go. One latte for mom and one white-chocolate milk for Ryan."

"Thanks." Ryan took a long drag from the to-go cup.

Mrs. Fletcher patted his head then turned her attention back to the espresso machines.

Cinnamon filled the air, soothing after such a traumatic morning. She took a sip then set it on the counter next to Ryan.

Cathy sashayed over to them with a broad smile. "You know, I'd be happy to watch Ryan for you. We'd have fun together. Right, kid? I bet we can even get Rebecca and Rusty to hang with us. I know she misses you after moving out of your house."

Ryan spun on his stool. "Yeah! Can we?"

A little weight of parental obligation lifted from Julia's shoulders. "Thank you. That would be nice. He misses Rebecca. We're happy for them both, but he definitely misses her living with us."

Cathy leaned close. "That's not the only reason I offered, darling. I think it's high time you got some 'me' time," Cathy air quoted.

"If you're implying I need to date, then you've lost so much weight that it's shrunk your brain cells." Julia shook her head. "No way. No how. I'm not ready for that. Besides, I don't have the time."

Cathy shifted and tilted her head to the side with her all-knowing brow lift. "That wasn't what I was referring to, but I think Mrs. Fletcher may have put some truth serum in your coffee. Sounds like you're the one who's missing companionship." She held up a hand to stall Julia's protest. "Not that it's any of my business. But who knows, maybe a man will just glide on past you one day and snag your attention."

Yeah, right. That was the last thing she needed. When Cathy West took someone on as a *project*, it meant trouble. Julia made a mental note to stay far away from Cathy for a while and hope she set her sights on someone else.

Cathy glanced over her shoulder then back at Julia. "I should probably return to Judy before she gnaws through the table waiting for her husband and their guest. But I'll see you later, little man." She winked at Ryan and he grinned.

"You ready, Ryan? I need to drop you at camp and then head to work."

"Yeess, maa'aam." Ryan's head drooped with defeat, but he hopped from the stool and snagged his white-chocolate milk. Julia offered her hand, but he stomped ahead and once more, she felt crushed under the weight of single parenting.

The front door opened and a gust of damp, warm air with a hint of cedar and manly cologne drew her attention. A man *glided* inside in a wheelchair. At one glance, she knew the man. A man with a flat top, dedicated gym time shoulders, jaw line chiseled by hard labor. A man of honor and code. A man dedicated to serving his country and who'd sacrificed both his legs for God and Country.

No, not a man. A hero. And she'd had enough of heroes.

CHAPTER TWO

T he smell of fresh ground coffee welcomed Doug Maverick Wilson into Café Bliss. A scent he used for morning motivation since he'd started working long hours restoring the home he'd recently purchased.

James scooted to the side and pointed to a table where Cathy West and Judy Benjamin already sat. Judy was all James talked about, when he wasn't trying to shrink Maverick's head.

With one glance at Cathy, he knew the woman was up to something. He'd only met her a handful of times since moving to Sweetwater County a few months ago, but she was easy to read. The darting gaze, pressed peach lips, and eyebrow calisthenics were all dead giveaways to a plot no doubt already in motion.

Why'd he agree to meet them here? All these people, not to mention whatever James was about to drop on him. James wanted something. He'd been as gentle as a tank rolling over eggs this morning when he'd picked Maverick up.

"What happened to you, mister?" a young boy asked.

Maverick glanced up to see a woman with legs that

stretched the length of any man's fantasy snag the little man by the shoulder. "Ryan, you know better than to ask such things."

A whiff of floral—lilac—broke through the strong aroma of coffee. It was refreshing to smell a light perfume after all the overpowering scents women typically wore. "No worries, ma'am. I'd rather people ask instead of trying to avoid looking at me."

The woman's cheeks tinged a pale pink and she shot a gaze at Cathy West. He'd been trained to read people, and judging by the way the woman clutched her bag and squared her shoulders, he knew the truth. Cathy, the town matchmaker, had plans for them. And by the narrowed I-can't-believe-you-did-this stare down, she felt the same as he did. Not interested.

He angled his chair at Ryan. "I had an accident that took both my legs, but I'm good now." His response sounded rehearsed and false from all the times he'd practiced it.

James squeezed his shoulder. "I'll be at the table when you're ready. Take your time."

Ryan shuffled between his size two feet. "My dad had an accident overseas, too."

The kid's words hit his chest like a concussion grenade. He'd prepared himself to face the widows and children left behind when soldiers died. But looking at this child was like facing down a jury. Did his dad lose his life because of a bad command? A command like the one he had made that cost so many of his comrades' lives.

"I'm sorry my son troubled you. Please excuse us."

The woman nudged her son toward the exit. The boy clopped a few feet with slumped shoulders and wobbly knees.

Maverick shook the haze away. "This chair isn't so bad, you know. I can go faster than most people can walk."

Ryan slid from the woman's grip. "Really? How fast you think you can go?"

"Ryan, don't badger the man," the woman scolded. Her flawless pale skin and high cheekbones could have been on the front page of one of those fashion magazines, but her eyes looked old and tired. Too old. Too tired. Too sad for someone her age.

The urge to pull her into his arms and make the pain go away filled him with surprise. Discreetly, his gaze swept the rest of her curves. Perfect. "It's fine. He's not badgering me." He looked down at Ryan. "Probably as fast as a car down a hill." Maverick angled his chair toward the woman. He wasn't interested in a relationship, but he'd be polite. Since moving to Creekside, he'd discovered that was the way things worked in small towns. "I'm Doug Maverick Wilson. You can call me Maverick. All my buddies do." He playfully slugged Ryan in the shoulder. "Maybe you can ride the chair down the hill one day. With your mom's permission, of course."

"Mr. Wilson, that's kind of you, but we need to be going." She avoided looking at his stumps for legs, the way every woman did, and turned on her worn black heel toward the door.

Ryan offered his hand to Maverick. "I'm Ryan and

that's my mom, Julia Cramer."

Maverick shook Ryan's hand. "It's a pleasure."

When he offered his hand to Julia, she politely smiled and shook it, but again, her eyes avoided looking below his neck. He accepted it though, the way women felt about him. It was penance for what he'd done.

"Nice to meet you, Mr. Wilson, but as I was saying, we need to be going." Her gaze traveled to his hand, to his face then to something behind him. Anywhere but his legs.

He rubbed stiffness from his chest, probably overdid it going up the hill on Main Street. "Gotcha. Well, little man, have a good day. I'll see you around."

"Awesome. I can't wait to go down that hill." Ryan pointed to the slope at the end of Main.

He didn't have a chance to say another word before Julia Cramer hustled her son from his sight.

"She's beautiful, isn't she?" Cathy said, walking over to stand beside him. "She's also smart and a good mother." She hip-bumped the handle of his chair, confirming his suspicions.

"No, thanks. Not interested." He shook off the aftereffects of whatever spell Julia Cramer had distracted him with then rolled between tables and chairs to where James and Judy sat. The last thing he wanted in his life was to be involved with a woman. Not to mention one who'd lost her husband at war.

"Do you want a coffee?" James asked.

He shimmied under the table and pushed his brakes down. "I'll get one, after you spill it."

"Spill it?" Judy asked, her perfect southern accent drawing out the syllables.

Maverick huffed. "I know you didn't ask me here for a morning coffee chat. James has an ulterior motive. So, what is it?"

Judy slid her purse to the side. "Oh, darling, you are perceptive. You see, we desperately need your help."

Help. The one word that pushed his inner Boy Scout button. "With what?"

James ran a sun-spotted finger around the perimeter of his coffee lid. "You owned a construction company back in Miami."

Maverick studied James and the way his gaze traveled to the ends of the table. "Yeah. And?"

James took a long sip then put his cup down but said nothing.

After a moment, Judy sighed. "My husband is trying to ask if you can help with a building project for charity. I'm afraid it wouldn't provide payment, though. The only budget we'll have is for operation expenses. We don't have money for building. It's all going to be done by volunteers."

"Ah, during our last session you said that I needed to concentrate on something. Is this really a charity thing for others, or for me?"

"Honey, you don't need charity. You're just fine on your own." Cathy pulled a chair out and sat. "You know, I was thinking. If this project works, we'll need someone to run things." She winked at Judy. "I've already spoken to the town council and there might be money in the budget to hire someone to run the building. Our lovely Julia Cramer would be perfect for the job and it would allow her to spend more time with her son. There wouldn't be a problem with him hanging out at the new facility, either."

Maverick sat military still, not wanting to say or do anything to encourage the woman.

She patted Maverick's hand. "She's such a lovely woman, and pretty, too. Don't you think?"

Judy swatted Cathy's hand. "You leave him alone. No one wants you playing matchmaker again."

The moment Cathy's attention shifted to Judy, he moved his hand off the table, resting it on the wheel of his chair.

James shook his head, his silver buzz cut shining under the lights. "When does Devon return from Virginia?"

Cathy gripped the edge of the faux-marble tabletop. "I know what you're implying, Mr. Benjamin, but if it wasn't for me—"

"We wouldn't be together." James nodded. "Yes, I know. The entire town knows."

Their bickering made a great distraction, so he unlocked his breaks and scooted away from the table. Rounding one of the black chairs, he wheeled over to the counter to order a coffee.

"Come on," Judy said, snagging Cathy's arm. "You promised to help me at the shop today. Let's go before you cause trouble. Maverick, I promise I'll keep her out of your way if you agree to help. The county sure could use your expertise."

Cathy shimmied out of her grip and huffed. "I was just tryin' to help."

The front door opened and a mass exodus of teens exited the coffee shop.

"Now maybe we can talk." James leaned back in his chair. "So, what do you say?"

Maverick gripped his black coffee then slowly rolled back toward the table. He had sold his business back home to escape the solemn looks from family and friends. But he missed it, missed working with his hands, building things, and watching them take shape before his eyes. This project would also give him a chance to help people, a way to atone for harming his men. And honestly, he'd do just about anything to get his mind off the war, his friends, and the military. "I'll do it. What's the charity?"

James scooted his chair to the left, effectively blocking Maverick's exit. "A center for returning veterans and military families."

A sandstorm of regret lashed Maverick's skin, just as raw and brutal as the real thing in the desert eight months earlier.

"I think it'd be a great opportunity for you, give you a chance to work on focusing on your strengths."

"Stop shrinking me. I'm not one of your PTSD patients, you know. I don't suffer from night terrors or anxiety."

"No, but men come back from war suffering from all different kind of things," James replied.

Maverick rubbed his forehead. That all too familiar pinching inside his temple warned a mortar fire headache was in route. If he wanted to get out of the coffee shop without sitting through another impromptu therapy session, he should just agree. Besides, working on a project and giving back wasn't such a bad idea. "I'll tell you what. If you stop digging into war wounds that don't exist then I'll help however I can."

James did his two finger *I've-gotcha* rub on his chin. "Sounds fair. I'll stop digging if you admit you're struggling with reintegrating into society."

"Listen, if you want me to do construction, I'm fine with that. But if you think I'm making excuses because I lost my legs in the war, I'm not. I've accepted it and I can do whatever you need. So, as you can see, no pity party here."

"Then why don't you use your legs?" James's words seared his lungs with fear.

"You serious?"

James dropped his hands to the tabletop. "Not the one's God gave you, the prosthetic ones. The ones you don't think you deserve to use."

CHAPTER THREE

The front door of Creekside Printing chimed the march of the last customer's exit. Julia eyed the large clock on the wall. It ticked down the last five minutes until she'd be able to head to Riverbend. To the nursing interview. To a new life.

Mr. Watermore, the owner of the printing shop, returned from his back office and approached the counter. "Mrs. Cramer, you know better than to have your heels off. We've spoken about this. You need to remain in your professional attire until the doors are locked and operating hours are over." A slow smile crept across his mouth. "Besides, with your legs, you should always wear heels."

A sick feeling stamped her stomach with warning. "I understand, but we shouldn't have any more customers, and my back's aching from standing all day."

Mr. Watermore shook his head, his orange comb-over falling into his eyes. "Why didn't you say so?" He placed his hands on the small of her back.

She froze then took a step to the side and retrieved her heels. "I'm fine. Don't trouble yourself."

Undeterred, he stepped closer and rotated his thumbs in small, creepy circles. "I don't mind. We don't want you to have to lose this job because of some physical issue. Not when you have that adorable little guy to care for."

Her back muscles tightened. It had been over a year since her husband's death, but any touch by another man inked a mark of betrayal on her heart. She scooted further to the side and plastered an *I'm-gonna-appease-you-so-I-don't-lose-my-job* smile on her face. "Better. Thanks. No need to worry. I won't be calling in any time soon. I can manage."

One of the machines beeped in the back, indicating it needed toner. She slipped her aching feet back into her shoes and moved to the storage closet to get another cartridge but Mr. Watermore squeezed her elbow, stopping her.

"Don't worry about that. I'll take care of it. You have an interview today, right?"

She fought the desire to elbow him in the chin. To tell him it wasn't okay to touch her, even if it appeared innocent. When her husband was alive, she had no problem establishing boundaries with men, but now it was different. She couldn't deck her boss because he touched her back or elbow. A paycheck meant more than her self-esteem, it paid for a roof and food for Ryan. And something told her if she directly forbade Mr. Watermore from touching her, she'd be out of a job. "Thanks. I appreciate it." She tugged her elbow from his hand and retrieved her purse.

"You know, people in this town care for you," he

said. "All this hard work and more school isn't necessary. If you had a man to take care of you, all your troubles would be over. You'd have more time for your son. After all, a mother should be home with her children."

His chauvinistic, parental advice pressed into her resolve, she wasn't about to put her son in the care of a man like him. She swallowed the lump of anxiety welling in her throat and slipped her purse strap over her shoulder. "Yes. Becca, Rusty, the Benjamins and of course, Cathy West have been amazing to me. Especially Cathy. People say she can ruin a person with her gossip, but I always found her charming."

"You're close to Cathy?" Mr. Watermore asked.

"Yes. She's tight with Becca so I see her all the time. She's amazing with Ryan, too."

His oversized bottom lip rolled over the top one in an ape-like pout. The air-conditioning cut on. Air swooshed from a vent overhead, flapping his hair up into an orangutan fluff. "You should be careful around that woman. When I opened this shop seven years ago, she made a huge fuss over my little sign out front."

That eyesore? The large neon *Creekside Printing* sign looked better suited to be advertising a strip club and blocked the scenic view from the top of the hill of downtown Creekside. She could imagine Cathy's matching purple complexion when she discovered the monstrosity. Maybe that was why Cathy barked her concern at Julia working here.

"I'll be careful." She slid around the counter, her heels echoing through the small, empty store, accentuating the fact she worked alone with a man she didn't trust. "I'll be here to open in the morning, so you can sleep in."

Mr. Watermore rocked back on his heels, his hands on his hips, chest pressed out, chin high. He was only missing the red hat and he'd be the spitting image of a garden gnome. "That's awfully sweet of you but I couldn't miss seeing your smiling face first thing in the morning. It's what I dream about all night."

His words sent her system into red alert, flushing her skin with anger. Anger at being trapped in a dead end job with a handsy boss, but knowing she couldn't do anything about it if she wanted to keep food on the table. What was worse was that he knew it, too. Jobs were too scarce in Sweetwater County, but she wouldn't give up the home she'd bought with Henry three years ago before he was deployed. Their dream was to raise Ryan in a small, family-friendly town, where neighbors cared for one another. Now she just felt trapped.

Julia dropped into her car and slammed the door, her skin still crawling with disgust and frustration. On the drive back into the heart of town, her skin slowly returned to normal, or as close to normal as the ninety-degree heat and a hundred percent humidity would allow. Luckily, her car's AC still worked, blowing icy air from the vents. She didn't want to think about what she'd do if that failed, too. As an uneducated widow and single mother, she couldn't afford even one more bill, however small, especially if it meant working for men like Mr. Watermore.

The long drive to the recreation center gave her

time to calm herself. Ryan had enough to deal with without worrying about her and she refused to burden him anymore than she already had. Even though Henry was dead, he deserved a stronger wife, someone who could care for his son. Ryan deserved a better life, with a mom who held it together and handled whatever came without complaint. And she deserved a life with a future. One that included less work and more time with Ryan, and not by marrying some man to take care of her. No, she'd manage to get into nursing school, earn her degree, and provide the life Henry and she had always wanted for Ryan.

She pulled into a parking spot, slung her purse over her shoulder, and headed inside to find Ryan. Hearing a faint vibration rumbling in her purse, she stopped in the lobby and retrieved her cell phone. A missed call. She wiped the humidity from the phone and recognized Mrs. Fletcher's number. Julia dialed voice mail and listened, a prickle of anticipation dotting the back of her neck.

"Hi, darling. I'm so sorry to do this, but I have a family emergency. I won't be able to watch Ryan this evening. I'm truly sorry. I hope you get this message in time—"

Julia didn't need to listen to the rest. The message was clear. She didn't have anyone to watch Ryan. Without a babysitter, she couldn't go to the interview for nursing school. If she missed the interview, she couldn't get in. And if she didn't get in, she was stuck working for Mr. Watermore, stuck with a leaky roof, and stuck with no hope of a brighter future. Just stuck.

*****

Evening light faded over the hilltops, the golden hue highlighting the wheat fields surrounding the Benjamin farm. Maverick veered onto the dirt cut-through road leading to the other side of the field where the abandoned government hanger sat.

Miles of wheat fields gave way to broken asphalt. His truck bounced over potholes and long crevices until he spotted the storage facility. It looked like a replica of some hidden nuclear experimental facility from World War II. What did James think he was going to do with it?

James stood outside the building in jeans, work boots, and a cap with a piece of wheat between his teeth, looking nothing like the psychiatrist he'd met at the VA in Miami over a year ago. He looked more like an old farmer.

Maverick pulled to a stop outside some side buildings resembling army barracks and shoved his door open. The evening air brought some relief from the hot summer day and he took a moment to let it wash over him. Then he yanked his wheelchair from behind his seat and lowered it to the ground.

James leaned against the driver door. "Hey, thanks for meeting me out here."

Maverick maneuvered down into his chair and wheeled around the front end of his Ford F-150. His left wheel caught on some rubble and jerked him to a halt. Dust and dirt spun, but his wheel didn't move.

Glancing up, he spotted James's judgmental gaze. "Don't start."

James shrugged and gave him a push. "Start what?"

"Telling me that if I used the prosthetic legs this kind of thing wouldn't happen. It would give me more freedom and accessibility."

A gust of wind rattled a metal shingle on the roof of the large storage building, producing an eerie moan that echoed over the open land.

James walked to the door and held it open. "I wasn't going to say anything, but since you brought it up... You know you'll need them if you're going to work construction again."

Maverick wheeled toward him but stopped shy of the doorway. "Who said anything about going back to construction? I don't need to work right now. I still have plenty of money to live off of from the sale of my business. Besides, I don't have the time. I volunteer at Rusty's delivery business to homebound people in Sweetwater County, and at the senior service center that Trianna Mason runs."

"It may not be paid work but you did agree to help with the construction of the Veterans project. And you'll be making Rusty's life a little easier. Not to mention you'll be working on your survivor's guilt at the same time."

"Subtle isn't one of your gifts, is it, shrinker?"

James kicked some bottles out of the way and waved Maverick inside. His wheelchair bumped over the threshold into a huge room. A room with beer bottles, graffitied walls, trash and an odor of bile and urine.

"Um, this needs more than construction. It needs a wrecking ball." He held his knuckles to his nose and examined the structure. It had solid wood beams and a strong metal roof that had survived numerous strong storms, but it needed drywall repair. Not to mention updates to the electrical and plumbing to bring it to current code requirements. That, and a good cleaning.

James climbed the side stairs and rattled the ironwork. "I think it's solid, but you're the expert."

"What are you hoping to do with this place?"

James stomped back to the floor. "Ah, that's an excellent question. I'm hoping to create a facility for our veterans, their family members. Anyone who's suffered in defense of our country's freedom."

Maverick fought the alluring call of country and duty. "This is where you want to have it?" He shook his head. "You trying to give those vets more nightmares? Besides, isn't helping Veterans and their families what the VA is for? You know, the place where you work?"

Wind blew the door shut and it bounced open again, startling them both. James sat on the second step so he was eye level with Maverick, a technique to make him feel like they were on the same level. James had used it numerous times since he'd returned from combat.

Maverick rolled to his side near the broken window, welcoming the fresh air.

James rested his elbows on his knees. "I only work there part-time. It was a favor from when they opened the PTSD clinic in Riverbend. They wanted me to help start it. I have, and now I'm ready to do something here in Creekside. There's a need for it here. Right now, anyone in this town and two towns to the east has to drive to Riverbend for help."

"You want to open a VA here?" Maverick shook his head. The man needed some head shrinking himself. Not only was that an impossible undertaking, Maverick didn't think there were enough veterans in all three towns to fill even a third of this building.

"No, nothing like that. I'm looking at offering more support services, counseling to returning veterans, widows, and families, and transition services for wounded soldiers returning home. You told me once that it was tough returning home and having to travel two hours from where you lived for rehab. If we can fix up the outer buildings, we can house people who are convalescing. I've already spoken with the VA and they are willing to provide transportation to and from Riverbend for Veterans that need medical attention."

"Do you really think there's a need for something like this here?"

James's right brow saluted. "Don't you?"

Maverick scanned the area once more, eyeing the outer buildings through the window. "I don't know. Maybe."

"Listen son. I know you're still struggling and you don't want to talk about it, but you need to move on with your life. You made it home. You have the right to live and move on."

The too-familiar gut-twisting sense of remorse

burrowed through his gut. "Do I?" James opened his mouth, but Maverick held up his hand. "Listen, shrinker. I don't have night sweats. I don't want to kill anyone, nor do I suffer from anger issues. I'm fine. I don't need PTSD therapy."

"No, you don't," James agreed.

"Good, then find another contractor." Maverick turned his back on James and wheeled toward the door. These men returning home from war needed someone right for the job, someone who made the right decisions and took care of them. And no amount of care and attention to these men would help him atone for the men he'd failed.

"You don't have PTSD but you do suffer from survivor's guilt. And this is your chance to help the men who suffered the way your men had suffered. Men who need your help, your qualifications, your abilities."

Maverick pushed his wheels faster. "Then they're screwed."

"Don't run away from this. You've been running long enough. Or should I say rolling."

Maverick swung around. "You don't know what you're talking about. It's easier in the chair, so stop thinking this so-called project is going to fix everything I've done. Trust me, there's no project big enough to repair the damage I caused my men and their families. They didn't get to come home, because of me."

"And because of you, new men will be able to live on with their families. All you have to do is choose to walk the path of healing."

Maverick squeezed the wheels of his chair. They

squealed under his grip, warning they'd pop if he continued. "Funny play on words, but it won't work. There's no way I could do a project like this. I can't reach high enough, I don't have the balance, and I certainly don't trust that I'd do it right."

Before he could make his escape, gravel crunched under car tires, drawing both of their attention to the asphalt runway outside.

Maverick released his protesting tires. "Bring reinforcements?"

"No," James said, heading outside. "No one knows I'm out here, except for Judy."

Maverick followed him out the door to find Judy, with little Ryan by her side.

"Hey. What are you doing here?" James kissed Judy's cheek.

"Julia had her big interview at Riverbend and Mrs. Fletcher had an emergency. So, I offered to hang with Ryan for a few hours. This was on our way home, so we thought we'd stop and check it out.

Ryan ran over to Maverick. "Hi! You gonna rebuild this place? Can I help?" The little boy shuffled between his feet, a light shining in his eyes that wasn't there earlier, a light of hope. "Mrs. B says you're gonna fix it up and I might have a place to go while my Mama's at school. When she's done with school she won't have to work two jobs and I can see her more." He ran past and stood on tiptoes to spy through the window. "That's so cool. Can I go inside?"

Maverick didn't know what to say. How would a kid understand why he didn't want to work on this place?

Judy gave him a sheepish look. "I might have told him that we were thinking of providing childcare to help our military wives be able to work to better their lives. Julia says she knows many women in her position. They try to help each other, but none of them can afford the time or money to help. They're all fighting to survive."

James slipped his arm around Judy's waist and guided her to Ryan. "That's an excellent idea. I think this place is going to change lives."

"I think it's going to save them," Judy said. Her hand slid onto Maverick's shoulder and squeezed the resistance from his body.

He watched Ryan run around the side of the building. "Be careful. There could be jagged metal," he called, but Ryan disappeared around the corner, Maverick huffed. "You two play dirty."

CHAPTER FOUR

The large brick structure stood tall with promise. But was she really ready for a university? Julia stood watching a bird soar over the clock tower and perch on a large antenna. People passed, book bags slung over their shoulders. To her relief, not all of them looked like infants, barely away from mom and dad for the first time.

She took a deep breath and climbed the front steps to the building marked *Administration*. On the other side of the glass doors, she discovered a long hall. It was clean and large. Too large. She'd only attended a junior college for one year. Then, when Ryan came along, she finished her second year online. Thank goodness Riverbend College existed. The thought of attending the University of Tennessee made her ribs shrink like a lab experiment gone wrong.

"Excuse me." Someone shuffled past, urging Julia to enter the administration office through another set of glass doors.

A young woman with bobbed brown hair stood up from behind a desk. "Are you Mrs. Cramer?"

Julia managed a nod, her words catching in her

throat along with the fresh aroma of a spring air freshener in the corner.

"Please, follow me. Dr. Mitchem Taylor, Dean of Nursing, is waiting for you. His son has a little league game this evening, so he's anxious to meet with you on time."

"Oh, am I late?"

"No, not at all." She gave Julia a warm smile. "Relax. Dr. Taylor's not the least bit intimidating. I've worked for him the last five years. He's been through a lot, but he's never let a student down." The woman offered her hand. "I'm sorry. Where are my manners? I'm Cynthia Gold, his administrative assistant."

"Julia Cramer, but I guess you already know that. It's nice to meet you." *Stop babbling,* her grandmother's words echoed in her head. A nervous habit she'd inherited from her mother, or so her grandmother had told her.

Cynthia led her down a long hall lined with offices. The names of professors and administrators adorned most of the doors on gold plates. "Just this way." Cynthia opened a door. "Dr. Taylor. I have Julia Cramer to see you now."

"Yes, yes. Send her in, please." The distinguished man stood and rounded his desk with a pleasant smile, not the Dean-of-school glare she'd anticipated.

The room looked old school, with the shelves of books, leather, dark hard woods, and an oriental rug.

"It's nice to meet you, sir," Julia said.

Dr. Taylor gestured to a leather chair angled in front of his desk. "Please, sit. I'd like to get started if that's okay with you."

Julia sat across from him and Cynthia closed the door, sealing Julia to her fate. "Yes. Thank you so much for accommodating my meeting time request. I'm sorry if I've made you late to your son's game."

"No, I'll make it in plenty of time. I try to make all of his games though, since his mother passed away two years ago. It's just him and I, so I make sure I'm there for him."

That look of loss, only another surviving parent could read and understand, shadowed his eyes. A little of the tension eased from her shoulders.

"Ah, are you a widow?" Dr. Taylor said.

Julia slid her purse strap off her shoulder and placed it in her lap. "You're very perceptive."

"It's my job." He crossed one of his long, muscular legs over the other, resting his foot on a knee. His pressed suit fit to perfection. "Do you have help with your son? Any grandparents to watch him while you take classes and study?"

Julia gripped the straps of her purse tight. She cleared her throat to hide the sadness that always crept in when she spoke of her parents. "No, I'm afraid not."

Dr. Taylor scratched his chin and his brows creased in question. "Did you lose them at an early age?"

Julia chuckled sadly. "You really are perceptive. Yes, my father died in Vietnam. I never knew him. My mother died when I was five. My grandmother raised me. I had a good life with her."

"I see. How old is your son?" he asked.

Julia wasn't sure why the man was asking such personal questions. She'd prepared for questions about her GPA, her study and organizational skills, why she chose nursing, and what her strengths and weaknesses were. "He's six. He'll be seven in a few weeks."

"So, he's not of age to remain home alone."

"No. He's not."

"Where is he now?" The man's voice wasn't accusatory, more like a concerned big brother. Still, it made her nervous. Would he refuse her admittance if he felt she didn't have sufficient childcare?

"He's with friends."

Dr. Taylor sat forward and clasped his hands together. "Will they be watching him while you're in classes at night for the next two years?"

"I'll have childcare set up for that. Don't worry. I'll make it work. I always do." Julia wasn't sure if she was trying to convince him or herself, but somehow this had to work out.

"Do you work, Mrs. Cramer?"

Finally, some questions she could use to steer the conversation to her strengths. "Yes, sir. I work two jobs. I'm an extremely hard worker. I graduated with a GPA of 3.98 from junior college, while raising my son. I've never called in sick a day in my life. I'm dedicated and you won't find another student more focused on learning. All I want to do is better my life for my son and myself. And I've always wanted to be a nurse, ever since I was a little girl."

The clock on the wall chimed seven times and Dr. Taylor glanced up at it. "I have no doubt you're a hard worker, Mrs. Cramer. You said you've wanted to be a nurse since you were a little girl. Why do you think that is?"

Julia searched for an answer, anything but the truth. If she shared the truth, she'd come across as damaged, a little girl trying to right a wrong. But the truth was all she ever had. "My mother died when I was home alone with her and I wasn't able to save her."

Dr. Taylor sat straight, his chin high. "I believe that's the most honest and heartfelt answer I've ever heard in the ten plus years I've been interviewing students. I have no doubt in my mind that you'll make an excellent nurse, Mrs. Cramer. Your resume and the references you provided prove you're intelligent, hardworking, dedicated, and have the heart of a nurse...but I do have a concern."

"What's that?" she asked. He eyed her hands twisting the straps of her purse into Twizzlers, so she released them and placed one on each armrest.

"How will you find time to study? I'm sure you'll find suitable daycare for your son, and I have no doubt you'll attend your classes, but this is a rigorous program, Mrs. Cramer. There'll be hours of study required to pass classes." Dr. Taylor stood and retrieved his briefcase from behind his desk.

Terrified the interview was already over, without her even having the chance to protest, Julia shot up, her purse falling to the floor with a loud thump. "I'll find a way."

He put his briefcase on the desk and rested his hands on top. "I tell you what. If you can manage to only work one job, not over forty hours, and prove you have appropriate childcare, I'll personally recommend you for the last remaining spot for the fall semester."

"I've already enrolled in my final two pre-requisite courses this summer semester. If I make straight A's, will you accept that?" Julia knew she could do it. Nothing stopped her when she set her mind to something. Her grandmother told her she got that trait from her dad.

"I don't think summer classes are a good idea, Mrs. Cramer. They are abbreviated semesters. You'll be putting yourself through even more stress. I've seen people break under less pressure. I don't want you to have a breakdown. Your son needs you."

Had he seen a file on her mother? Did he know how she died? Is that where his concern came from? Well, that wasn't Julia. She'd show him. "I'll be fine. And when I make straight A's and do it without having a nervous breakdown, then you'll recommend me for the remaining spot in the program." Julia held out her hand. "I'm glad we agree. I'll let you get to your son's game now. I've taken up too much of your time already."

Dr. Taylor chuckled. "You're determined, I see. Just promise me, if you're struggling, that you'll drop your classes and allow yourself some time. You could take prerequisites in the fall and then start the next year."

"I appreciate your concern, but I'll be fine." Julia lifted her hand a little higher and he took it. She knew the man would keep his word. Knew it from the picture on his desk next to the one of his late wife and his son in a baseball uniform. It was a picture of him with his men crouching beside a beige hummer in an equally beige landscape. He was a man who followed a code, the same code her Henry had followed.

Now, she needed to figure out how to make straight A's, keep Ryan happy, pay the bills, and not die from exhaustion.

CHAPTER FIVE

Ryan ran laps around Judy Benjamin's farmhouse table, having already defeated both James and Judy in a game of catch-me-if-you-can. Maverick caught him mid-stride. "I win," he declared triumphantly as Ryan burst into giggles.

Judy leaned against the doorway to the kitchen. "I guess I better start exercising if I'm going to keep up with my granddaughter when she gets to be your age."

Ryan crinkled his nose. "Girls don't play like this. They're boring. Except for one girl at camp. She throws a football better than me."

James clapped his hand to his thigh and howled with laughter. "Sounds like our little man is all boy. I was just like him when I was his age."

"Oh, Lord. I hope he's nothing like you. If I remember correctly, you pushed Cathy into the mud in her new white dress on Easter Sunday when we were nine." She shook her head. "Your mother looked like she'd swallowed fire."

"My butt felt like she had by the time my dad came home. I think I still feel the sting when I sit down. But I didn't deserve it," James said.

Maverick plopped Ryan on his lap and wheeled into the living room, forcing James and Judy out of his way.

"What do you mean you didn't deserve it?" Judy protested. "Cathy went home crying because you ruined her dress."

"Yes, but I did it to save your honor. She'd pulled your hair, so I pushed her. Don't you remember?"

Maverick settled in the corner of the parlor near the window and Ryan climbed onto the satin covered gold chair beside him, the boy's eyes already glued to the TV. He listened to them bicker playfully over memories of their childhood, a little envious at the deep bond they shared. Before he went to war, he thought he'd found his lifetime mate, too. But when he returned with missing limbs, Barbara couldn't handle it. He didn't blame her, though.

A car rumbled up the drive.

Ryan leaned against the back of the chair and pulled the white lace curtains to the side. "Mom!" he yelled then leapt from the chair and raced out the front door.

Maverick maneuvered around the large antique couch and headed after him. "Ryan. Stay on the porch. It's dark."

"Yes, sir." Ryan bounced impatiently on the top step.

Fireflies danced in the darkness over the open field. Maverick rolled forward then gently nudged the back of Ryan's leg with his front wheel. "Hey, you want to go catch fireflies one night? We could put them in a jar as a nightlight."

Ryan's face lit up, only to go blank a moment later. "You can't do that."

"Why not?" Maverick asked.

"Because you ain't got no legs. You can't go chasing anything."

Maverick swiveled in a circle and popped a wheeler. "Sure, I can."

"Hey, you weren't going to leave without saying goodbye, were you?" James tapped Ryan on the head. "Besides, we've got to show your mother what you made today with Ms. Judy."

"Oh, yeah." Ryan ran back inside while Julia made her way up the front steps.

She looked tired. Of course she was tired. She'd worked all day then drove to Riverbend for an interview. The woman never stopped. She pushed strawberry blond hair from her emerald eyes. He hadn't noticed them earlier. How could he have missed them? Maybe because he wasn't distracted by her legs and curves this time.

"Sorry I'm late. I didn't mean to intrude on your company."

"Who? Him? He's not company." James smacked Maverick on the shoulder. "Come on in. Ryan wants to show you something."

"Okay, but only for a minute. I need to put Ryan to bed and then get to work."

Maverick spun around to follow. She sidestepped to allow him to pass, but he halted and directed her forward. She nodded awkwardly. The chair tended to make people uncomfortable. He didn't mind, though. It always reminded him of the men who didn't make it home. "Didn't you already work today? I didn't know the printing shop was open at night."

"How'd you know I work there?" Julia put her purse on the coat rack in the entryway.

Maverick shrugged. "I think Cathy mentioned it to me earlier."

Julia smiled, a hint of happiness to it. Not a full-blown smile, but he'd take it. "I see. Well, she neglected to mention that I also work for her. I mend clothing at night. It's what pays for camp for Ryan. She's doing me a favor sending work my way."

"Come into the kitchen, you two," Judy called.

"So, you work a second job just to pay for that? Can you find another job that'll cover your normal expenses and day camp?"

"Not around here," Julia replied stiffly. An indication it was time to back off. "Besides, Ryan loves day camp. He'd rather be there than with me."

"No, I wouldn't." Ryan sat on his knees in a dining chair so he could reach the middle of the table. He shoved something wrapped in white paper at Julia.

"You're right. Being at home with you is the best." She gave the boy a big squeeze. "But since I can't have you at work with me, honey, camp is the next best thing, right? I wish I could be with you all the time, but there's no job in Creekside that I can do full time from home, or that would allow you to be by my side. If there was, I'd quit my job at the print shop immediately. Trust me." Julia unwrapped three cookies, chock full with nuts, chocolate and other lumps no one could identify. Yet, the suspicious lumps didn't seem to deter her. "Wow. You did this all by yourself?"

"Yeah-huh," Ryan nodded faster than a woodpecker. "I can't wait to eat them later. Thanks."

James pulled out a chair for her. "Please sit."

Julia lowered into the chair and Maverick rolled under the table to her left. "I think we're being ambushed," he whispered to her. "I'm not allowed to leave either. James even removed the ramp out front to keep me here."

"I did no such thing," James scolded.

"Okay, but Judy said she'd never make her apple cobbler for me again if I left."

Judy joined them at the table. "That's true. I did say that."

James kissed the top of her head. "I knew I loved you. Trust me, Maverick. When you find the right woman, never let her go."

Maverick shifted in his chair. If he had any doubts earlier about them scheming to get Julia and him together, they were gone. *God, James really needs to work on his subtly.* Relationships weren't in his future. Not that he didn't think the woman by his side was attractive, and that her kid wasn't amazing. But that wasn't the life he was meant to have.

Julia elbowed him in the side. "I guess we better listen. I'm not risking Judy's apple cobbler, either."

Her playful smile drew his attention and a warmth surrounded his chest. He wanted to do something to make this woman joke again, to be happy for a moment longer, before she returned to being the tired, unhappy creature she was when she walked in.

Ryan shook his head. "You best not. It's awesome."

Judy hugged him. "I'll never keep my apple cobbler from you. Even if your mother is grounded."

"Great," Julia giggled. "He's gonna hold that over my head for weeks. You just made my son very happy." Her smile lit the room once more.

Ryan bounced in the chair on the other side of her. "You said my mom might be able to be home with me insteada working?"

James leaned back in the chair at the end of the table. "Not exactly."

Ryan slumped. "Oh."

Maverick prepared himself for another argument. He'd thought about it all day, and there was no way he'd take on this project. He'd be a hypocrite working to save veterans and their families, after causing so many deaths. His hands trembled at the memory, so he rested them on the end of his stumps. A reminder that he deserved his situation, if not worse.

"Listen, little man," James said. "We're gonna need your help, too."

Ryan sat up tall. "Really?"

"Really." James took Judy's hand in his. "We were talking and we think it's time to bring everyone into this project."

Julia looked to Maverick. "I don't understand. What project?"

Maverick shrugged, feigning ignorance. He'd hoped to escape before she arrived.

Judy cleared her throat. "We've been able to arrange a new facility for veterans and their families here in Creekside. In recent years, we've had so many soldiers return home in need of so much. Not to mention their families."

Maverick felt the heat of Julia's gaze penetrating him, but he couldn't face her, not about this. Not when her husband had died at war. Not with such a high death toll on his conscience.

"Okay, but I don't know what this has to do with me," Julia said. Her voice quivered and he wanted to take her hand in his, to reassure her things would be okay. But that was a promise he couldn't make.

"If this all works out, there'll be a job there. A job where Ryan can go with you each day when he's not in school."

Ryan gasped. "I wouldn't have to go to that silly baby camp anymore?"

Julia dropped her hands onto her table. "I didn't know you felt that way."

Ryan did a one-shoulder shrug. "Like you always say, there's no reason to complain. Only reason to work to change something."

Julia rubbed her temple. "I guess I do say that."

Maverick leaned toward Julia and lifted a hand to her petite arm, but pulled it away at the last moment. "It sounds like that doesn't matter. There's a job for you, so things can change."

Julia lowered her hands and looked at him. Her eyes were red and dark circles surrounded them, but still she looked good. "Things don't change. Not like that. Not that easy. You heard Judy. There *might* be a job, and I can't stake our future on a might."

"Let me explain," Judy said. "There are funds

already in place. The city council has established a position, half of the salary will be provided by the county. The other half is being provided by a three-year stipend that Trianna Mason was able to acquire through a grant. She's become a wiz with grant applications since she started running the senior center. The job will be to organize the day-to-day affairs of the facility, something you'll have no trouble with. And since James, Cathy, and I will be on the board overseeing this project, we'll have final say in who's hired. Our choice would be you. We believe you've demonstrated the ability to handle difficult situations while dealing with multiple issues. You're well organized and you're studying to be a nurse."

"Maybe," Julia said, her voice sounding hallow, foreign.

Judy cupped her hand over her mouth. "Oh, I'm so sorry. We were so excited about the job opportunity, and what this program would mean for the county, that we never asked about the interview. To be honest, I just assumed you'd ace it."

"It was fine." Julia shrugged. "I might be granted access, but I'm afraid I made some promises to get ma I might not be able to keep."

"What did you promise?" Judy asked.

Julia's eyelid twitched and he worried she'd start crying. He didn't think his heart could take seeing her with tears. "I'll have to make straight A's on my college classes this summer, while working both jobs. And I don't want to neglect Ryan. If I don't make straight A's, Dr. Taylor will refuse my entrance."

"Really?" James's eyebrows rose nearly to his hairline. "That doesn't sound like Dr. Taylor. I know him. He's a dedicated professional and a good man. I've worked with him on some research that he conducted about veterans' preparation for war and proper after-battle screening. I'll talk to him on your behalf."

Maverick swallowed the raw lump of regret and forced his mind to remain in the present.

Julia shook her head. "No, thank you. If I'm going to get into the school, it'll be on my own merit."

Maverick cupped her hand before his mind caught up with his body. "But it sounds like you won't need to work two jobs now."

She didn't pull away. Her hand remained in his and he thought he'd jump out of his chair and dance around the table on his stumps. Not that he could dance even before he lost his legs.

"You said I *might* have a job. You've told me all the reasons I would be great at it, and that you're dead set on hiring me. So, where does the *might* come in?"

"We have all the donated supplies, the money from the VA, county, city, and grants, but we don't have a builder. And it's not in the budget to pay one."

"Oh, I see." Her hand pulled from his, taking his resolve with it.

"That won't be a problem," he said, gripping the arm of his chair. "I'll volunteer."

CHAPTER SIX

Was it true? Would she really be able to leave her job at Creekside Printing? Exchange her heels for sneakers? Not have to fend off advances from Mr. Watermore every time she turned around? Would she really see more of Ryan and have to work less? She flung her arms around Maverick. "Thank you."

"Um, sure." He patted her arm and she realized she was hugging a strange man. Yet, she hadn't run screaming from the room, and that ugly feeling of betrayal didn't plague her. Was it because James and Judy seemed to trust him?

She unwrapped herself and scooted away. "Ah...sorry."

"No need to apologize. I'm not complaining." He looked away, but she swore she saw him blush. Could a man, a soldier, blush from a simple hug? He was a good-looking man—blond, stormy grey eyes—any woman's dream of the perfect leading man in their world. She shook her head. What the heck was she thinking? What had gotten into her?

"So, when do you think this job will become available?" Julia straightened her suit jacket.

"Anxious, are we?" Judy teased. "It depends on how long repairs to the buildings take. The grant money will start thirty days prior to opening."

Maverick ran a hand over his crew cut. He looked like James's son in a way, with the same soldier-like posture and short hair. "There's a lot to be done. Will we be able to wrangle some volunteers?"

James nodded. "Not a problem. I already have a few people in mind."

Julia looked between them. "So? How long?"

"If we don't have to do anything structural, and I can't guarantee that my five minutes of looking over the building would suffice as an inspection, then we might be able to finish in forty-five to sixty days, depending on volunteer help."

"That means I'd only have to work at the print shop for another few weeks." She couldn't hide her excitement. Everything had changed in an instant. Life didn't treat her well, it never had, but for her son, she would go for it. Anything for Ryan and their future.

"Are things not going well at the print shop? Cathy's been worried about Mr. Watermore and his roaming hands."

"What?" Maverick's voice boomed through the house. He cleared his throat. "That's harassment."

"What's harassment, Mama?" Ryan asked.

Julia stood and rounded the table, taking Ryan into her arms. "Nothing for you to worry about. It just means he bothers me sometimes, but it's nothing I can't handle."

Ryan swiped bangs from his eyes. "You mean like

Mean Mike teases me at camp?"

"Yes. Something like that." Julia kissed his forehead.

"Then I don't like him. I want you to stop working there. If I help, can you stop sooner?" Ryan pushed from her arms and rounded the table to Maverick. His large eyes were transfixed, worshiping. He couldn't be that attached to the man already. They'd just met this morning. Of course, when Rusty came to fix a few things around their house, Ryan had followed him around from the moment he walked through the door.

"It's okay. We won't let anyone hurt your mom. I promise." Maverick lifted Ryan onto his lap, like a father would lift a son.

No way. She wouldn't allow Ryan to fall for the hero. Heroes were only men on high pedestals that broke when they fell. "We better get going, Ryan." She lifted her son from Maverick's arms and led him to the parlor. "It's getting late, and I still have work to do tonight, and you have camp in the morning."

"Please, Mama. Can't I help with the construction? I don't want to go back to camp."

Julia snagged her purse from the coat rack. "Don't argue with me, honey. It's not safe for a child on a construction site." She glanced at James, Judy and Maverick hovering at the door. "I don't even know where this is going to be."

James held Judy close to his side. "My lovely wife came up with the idea. We'll be working out of the abandoned airfield. There's plenty of room for growth."

"That old place? Isn't it a pile of rubble by now?"

Julia asked, hoping she was wrong. Turning that place into a safe and working facility would surely take more than a few volunteers and a couple of weeks.

"No, it's still standing. The building was constructed back when they were worried about bombings, so the structure's still sound. It's just a little rough around the edges."

Maverick wheeled around James and Judy to Ryan. "Your mother's right. It's not safe for you to hang out there right now, but once we're done with the construction you'll be out there with your mom all the time."

"Wait. I have an idea. Ryan, would you like to help me in the garden tomorrow?" James asked. "I could sure use your help."

"Can I, Mama?" Ryan danced between his feet. "Pleeaase?"

"I can't ask the Benjamins to watch you all day. That's not fair to them. They have other things to do."

"You're right," Judy agreed, nodding solemnly. "We wouldn't want him for a day. We want him every day. He'll be good practice for us to prepare for Amelia when she gets older."

"Really? Really?" Ryan squealed.

Maverick fist-bumped him. "Sounds like you have other plans than hanging with Mean Mike tomorrow."

Julia stared at them. No. When did this happen? True, the man was breathtaking, with his strong arms, firm chest, and child-like personality. But she couldn't let this happen. Ryan couldn't fall for another hero. She couldn't fall for another hero. She had to keep her son, and herself, far away from him.

CHAPTER SEVEN

The sign at the boundary of Creekside welcomed Maverick as he maneuvered his truck onto the main strip leading into downtown. *Welcome to Sweetwater County. Where Your Heart and Home Belong*, the sign read. He liked that. He knew it didn't apply to him, but still it was nice.

A warm breeze raked over his skin through the open driver's side window, swished around the cab then left out the passenger side. As he slowed, so did the breeze, but the aromas of fresh flowers and food filled the air.

He pulled into a parking spot in front of J and L Antiques and sighed. A kind of contentment he hadn't felt before surrounded him, a quietness that leaked into his soul. Yellow and purple blooms tumbled over the sides of hanging baskets strung from the old-fashioned light posts.

Quiet, calm, beautiful, with a hint of strength. That was what Creekside represented, and Julia Cramer fit better than a general's pressed uniform. He shook his head, freeing his mind from the fog invading his well-planned bachelor life.

A hand hit the side of his open window. The sound of metal clanking against metal echoed through his ear, igniting the engine in his chest. His hand moved automatically to his hip before he realized he wasn't armed.

"Hey. You going to sit in that car all day, or we going to discuss plans for the complex?"

"Christ, old man. You claim to be some bigwig PTSD doc, but that was a bonehead move. I could've shot you before I thought about it."

James clanked his ring against the door three more times. "You don't suffer from PTSD, remember?"

"Don't even start, head-shrinker. Not if you want me on this project."

James lifted his hands in surrender. "I was just saying hello."

"Sure." Maverick shoved the door open, flipped his wheelchair out, and settled into it.

"But if I *was* going to head-shrink you, I'd ask you why you're not using your prosthetic legs again." James hopped up on the sidewalk and eyed the large step.

Maverick grunted, popped a wheelie, and rolled up onto the sidewalk. "Guess I don't need them."

"Whatever you say. I'm off duty today." James opened the door, but slid in first and let it swing shut behind him.

Maverick only shook his head, not willing to give James a chance to dig further into his choice not to use his prosthetic legs. He was looking for some reason that wasn't there. He just liked the wheelchair better. He swung the door open and slid inside before it could close on him. "And I thought the people of Creekside had manners."

Spices and fruity scents greeted him. J and L Antiques housed so many unique and beautiful pieces of furniture and knickknacks. Nothing like his half-finished home on the edge of town with patched white walls and sanded floors still waiting to be stained.

Judy rounded the counter and smacked James on the shoulder. "I saw what you did. Don't deny it."

James shrugged, kissed Judy on the cheek, and faced Maverick. "You said you didn't need any help. I thought it'd be an insult if I held the door open. I wouldn't want to insult the man who's going to pull this project up. I promised no psychobabble and no extra help."

"There are other ways to head-shrink, without talking. Just know I'm not fooled at all, old man."

Judy pulled a chair out of the way at a large wooden table. "Here. Not all us Benjamins are rude."

Architectural plans covered the tabletop. Curious, Maverick wheeled under and began analyzing them. Some were old and yellowed others new and freshly printed. After several minutes, he had a good idea of the structural changes. "If you want to take out this wall, we'll need to make sure it's not load bearing. And here you want to add several rooms. They should be on the other wall where there are already existing windows. We can utilize that natural light then put the open area here, where there is the one large upper window. Also, we'll need a plumber to give us an estimate on these additional bathrooms."

James sat across from him. "See, Judy? I told you we had the right man for the job."

Judy pointed at the center room they'd be adding in the old hanger. "That's where Julia's office will be."

Maverick eyed the small room with a tiny window that looked out onto the wall of the first barrack. "She won't have much light there." He scanned the plans and made a few notes. "Here, in the back corner. It overlooks the fields, has plenty of natural light, and we can widen this enough for her to place two desks and a few chairs. She'll need extra space for meetings, so we can put a conference table in this adjacent room. It could be multi-functional. We could add some toys and a computer. You know, veterans have families. If you want this to work, and you're serious about not only helping veterans, but educating their families about their challenges, then this would make more sense."

Judy leaned back, her hands on her hips with that Judy Benjamin you're-not-fooling-me eyebrow lift. "Mmmm-hmmm."

He ignored her tone and shuffled the papers around to look at the barrack-style housing. "I understand the use of this space and it makes sense, but I'd urge you to rethink the layout, or construction. It too closely resembles military barracks. In some ways this could be good for a transitional housing, but I'd like to help the men adapt to more normal surroundings."

"I was thinking the same thing." James nodded.

"Well, we can't afford anymore structural changes." Judy sighed. "I'll go make us some fresh iced tea while we think it over. I like your idea about Julia's office, though." She winked before making her way to the kitchen behind the mahogany counter.

Julia's office still didn't seem big enough, or airy enough, but he had to work with an old building and little resources.

James sat back in his chair. "I know I'm not supposed to work today, but can I ask you a friendly question. You know, buddy to buddy?"

Maverick ignored the warning siren sounding in his head. James had proven himself a friend, so how could he refuse him? "Okay."

"Your eyes lit up when Julia came to pick up Ryan yesterday. Not to mention that boy's enamored by you. They're good people, you know."

Maverick scooted back from the table and angled his chair to face James. "Don't even go there. No playing matchmaker. I'm a bachelor and I like it that way."

"I wasn't going to talk to you about Julia. I wanted to know what you thought about heading up the mentoring program for children left behind after their fathers and mothers are killed in action."

Maverick fidgeted with his breaks. "Oh. I thought you were trying to get me interested in Julia."

James shrugged. "What's wrong with Julia? Don't you think she's pretty?"

"Sure. Any man would."

James angled his head to the side. "But she's probably too strong for a guy like you. Most military men like their women more submissive."

Maverick laughed. "Submissive? You're ex-military. Would you call Judy submissive?"

James groaned in mock aggravation. "No. Judy is many things but submissive definitely isn't one of them. Guess that makes me an oddball," he chuckled.

"Then that makes two of us, old man. I prefer a woman with a backbone."

James smiled. "Oh, then it's because she has a kid."

Maverick shook his head. "No, I like Ryan. Heck, I love kids. Always wanted some of my own. Before the war, anyway."

"Then you just don't like her."

"I didn't say that." Maverick gripped the wheels of his chairs. "Stop putting words in my mouth. I'm not interested, end of story. So, you won't get under my skin, no matter what you say."

"Oh, I misread you then. I thought you were upset about Mr. Watermore and how he makes passes at her all the time. Heck, always making her wear heels because he likes her legs. Not to mention the constant phone calls to her late at night and his finding excuses to touch her."

"Any man would be offended if they heard of a woman being treated in such a way. That doesn't mean I have feelings for Julia."

"Then why are you about to pop the wheel on your chair?"

Maverick looked at his blanched hands, rubber oozing between his fingers. He released the wheels. "I just don't like men who harass women. It has nothing to do with Julia specifically."

The kitchen door swung open and Judy set a tray with a pitcher of iced tea and three glasses down on the table. "What were you two talking about? It looks serious."

"Nothing. Maverick was just explaining that he wasn't interested in Julia in a romantic way."

Judy poured tea into each cup, ice cubes tumbling in and splashing some liquid onto the tray. "Oh, good," Judy said.

"Good? Why?" Maverick bit his lip. What did it matter?

"Because Sam at the recreation center asked me if I'd set them up. I told him I'd think about it. I guess there's no reason to say no." Judy handed Maverick a glass.

He sipped, tasting a hint of apricot. His stomach churned with a nervous flutter he didn't understand. Had he met Sam? What kind of a man was he?

Maverick set his glass down, but kept his eyes transfixed on the small bubbles clinging to the ice cubes. "I don't remember meeting a Sam."

"You probably haven't. He's only been here a few weeks. Transferred from Riverbend. He races cars, runs an online business for extra money, and is recently divorced."

That churning boiled over into a steam of concern. "Doesn't sound like a good influence for Ryan."

Judy cleared her throat. "I thought you didn't care."

CHAPTER EIGHT

The summer humidity cloaked Julia in a hot, damp cocoon. Her clothes clung to her and no matter how often she washed her hands she just felt sticky. She longed to skip work and take Ryan to the lake. It had been so long since they'd gone, but when Henry was alive, they went often sharing many happy days there. The 4th of July picnic was only a few weeks away, one of their favorite holidays, but she didn't see how she could take Ryan to watch the fireworks, the barbeque and swimming. Not with her current workload. Besides, it wouldn't be the same without Henry.

"Mama, I don't think you should go to that job today."

Julia opened the passenger door to her old clunker and ushered Ryan into his seat. "You know I have to, buddy. It's the only way to pay the bills. I'd like to spend the day with you, but I can't." Julia shut the door then rounded the car, placing last night's sewing work on the back seat.

"It's not that. I don't want that man touching you. Dad's gone, so it's my job to protect you now."

Julia's heart tightened, his words sounding so much like something Henry would say. In their short time together, he'd taught Ryan about the importance of respecting and caring for women. She leaned across the seat and gave him a squeeze. "You know, Daddy would be proud of the young man you've become."

"He would?" Ryan clutched his backpack to his chest and stared out the window. "Mr. Maverick told me I was right to want to protect you. That's what sons did for their Mamas."

The mention of Maverick churned her insides. She sat still for a moment, thinking about all that had happened yesterday, and the promises of a better tomorrow.

Julia started the car and headed toward J and L Antiques to deliver her work to Cathy before dropping Ryan off at with James and heading to her day job. Cathy helped at the shop a couple days a week so Judy's partner and daughter-in-law, Lisa, could care for her little girl who was recovering from an illness.

As she drove, her mind kept replaying the events at the Benjamin farm. The way her son connected with Maverick, probably even more than he had to Rusty. But was that a good thing?

"Do you think Daddy would be upset if I ever got a new daddy?"

Julia swerved and an oncoming car honked. She shot her arm across Ryan's chest.

Several calming breaths later, she glanced at her son and his expectant gaze. She searched for an answer, but nothing sounded right. "You remind me a lot of him. The way you smile, with the right side of your bottom lip a little higher than the left. The way you scratch your ear when you're thinking about something important. The way you're always ready to protect the people you love."

Ryan pushed his shoulders back and lifted his chin, just like a little soldier. The same way he'd raised it when he'd placed the flower on his dad's casket. For such a young boy, he acted decades beyond his years.

He wanted to be a man, but he was only a boy. And she knew what she had to tell him, what Henry would've wanted. "I think your father would want you to have a man in your life to help you grow up. There's nothing wrong with you wanting a father figure in your life."

"Oh, so more of a big brother." His head lowered.

She knew she should correct him, tell him that wasn't what she meant, but deep down she knew it was. Henry was the saint, not her. "You know, I hear Becca's going to come by on her lunch break today. She's supposed to meet with Judy and Cathy about the 4th of July picnic planning." Julia steered onto Main and spotted the antique store ahead, a large truck, the one from the Benjamin farm parked out front. Her stomach fluttered and she gulped at the realization that the man named Maverick had wheeled his way into her thoughts.

"Will Rusty be there, too?"

Julia rubbed her clenched hands over the rubber-covered steering wheel. "Becca told me he insisted on coming by so he could see you."

"That's awesome. I'm going to have an amazing day. Between spending time at the farm helpin' Mr. B and hanging with Rusty. I don't think it could get any better. Well, unless you were there."

She pulled into the only spot, next to the large truck, and turned off the car. "You know I'd be with you if I could."

"That's okay. As long as that man doesn't bother you at work. Besides, we'll get to go to the lake soon." His wide eyes and broad smile faded. "I mean, if you want to go."

Did she? Did she want to celebrate a holiday where everyone rejoiced about their freedom, forgetting the lives lost to make it all possible? She often wondered if freedom came with too high of a price. A price she wished Henry hadn't paid. "If you want to then I want to."

"I want to."

"Then we'll go."

Ryan threw himself into her arms and hugged her tight. "You're double-stuffed awesome."

"And you're double-stuffed trouble."

Ryan play-smacked her. "Mama!"

"Oh, don't worry. You're still my favorite son."

"I'm your only son." Ryan laughed and hopped out of the car. "You best stop calling me your favorite. Someday, I'll have a little brother or sister."

Julia stumbled up onto the sidewalk, twisting her ankle, the clothes in her arms tumbling to the concrete.

"Mama. You okay?" Ryan darted to her side.

"Yes, I'm fine. Apparently, this is Shock-Your-

Mother day." She grabbed the hood of the car and hoisted herself back up on her stilts. Ugh, she hated wearing heels. She'd much prefer sandals, or boots.

"You sure? I can get help." Ryan shifted between his feet and held tight to her arm.

"I'm fine. No need to worry."

His face twisted in anguish. Too much anguish for a simple fall. "I'm fine. Really. Are you okay?" She squeezed his hand and pulled him into a hug.

Ryan shrugged. "Yeah, I was just worried about you. You sure you have to go to work today?"

Julia held him for that extra *mother second.* "I'm afraid so."

Ryan stepped away, his head hanging low. She wanted to ask him what really bothered him, but based on his slumped posture and wayward gaze, this wasn't sidewalk talk. "Hey. After work, let's grab a pizza and cupcakes and have a picnic on our living room floor."

Ryan lit up like the Sweetwater Fireworks display. "Really?"

"Really." Julia took his small hand and headed inside J and L Antiques. Each step she took eased the pain in her ankle a little, but she had to fight not to limp.

The inside of the antique shop always filled her with that cozy, welcome-home feeling. Cinnamon, nutmeg, and apple aromas tantalized her nose and she took in a long whiff. She longed to take her heels off and walk over the white bearskin rug over by the wood carved mantel. The door's jingling bell stopped and the room fell silent. She glanced at the three faces staring at her and Ryan. James and Judy smiled at her. Maverick... Maverick didn't smile. He didn't frown either. It was more of a look of facial paralysis.

Did she rip her skirt when she fell or something? She glanced down, but despite a small stain that had been there the last three months; there was no sign of her clumsy dance out front.

"Hi, Ryan," James called. "Are you ready for some hard work today?"

"You bet I am," Ryan said with an enthusiasm that rivaled Christmas morning.

Judy waved them over, but still Maverick sat with a frozen face, his gaze fixed on her every move. "Come. Sit and have some iced tea with us. It's gonna be one hot day today."

Julia set her work down on the table. "That's kind of you, but I can't. I need to get to work. Would you mind seeing that Cathy gets these? She said she'd drop by around ten to pick them up."

"Sure, hon. I'd be glad to. You sure you can't stay for a little bit?"

"No. Mr. Watermore would dock my pay if I'm late, and I don't want to lose any money. I have big plans later. I have an amazing date planned."

Maverick shifted, his face no longer frozen.

"Date? Oh, that's wonderful, hon. Isn't it?" Judy bumped into Maverick's shoulder.

"Yeah, sure. Except who's gonna be with Ryan?" His accusatory tone knocked the gushy feeling in her belly out and replaced it with a fire that matched the rising temperature outside.

"Me," she replied flatly. "He's my date." Julia clasped her keys so tight the jagged edge hurt her palm. "I don't like leaving my son, but some of us have to work." She spun on her heel, ignoring the protest of her right ankle, and kissed the top of Ryan's head. "You be good for Mr. Benjamin today. I'll head straight to get you the minute I can leave the print shop, okay?"

"Okay." Ryan kissed her cheek and disappeared to the other side of Maverick, firing off gardening questions at James.

Maverick cleared his throat. "I...I didn't mean..." He shook his head and eyed James, as if a secret lived between them. "You obviously have to work, but I'm not sure that print shop is the best place."

"Well, it's the only place I've got right now. The sooner you get your part done on that project, the sooner I can leave the printing shop and be with my son more."

Maverick chuckled, his face relaxing into a carefree smile. "No pressure."

The mantel clock chimed nine times, so she gave Ryan a quick hug. "I've got to go. I'll see you a little after five. Okay, bud?"

"Okay. I'll double-stuff miss you."

"I'll double-stuff miss you, too."

Julia walked out of J and L Antiques, leaving a little piece of herself behind. She hobbled to her car and drove the few blocks to Creekside Printing, hoping to beat Mr. Watermore. If not, he'd dock her pay thirty minutes for being three minutes late. Unfortunately, his little red sports car already sat in the handicap spot in front of the building. *Great.* The best thing for her to do was accept the loss of wages and get to work. Arguing about it never worked, and always invited him to come too close to her for comfort. It was best to keep her distance and concentrate on work.

She hopped from her car onto a wobbly ankle and the ache intensified. Favoring that leg, she hurried inside. Within seconds, Mr. Watermore stood in the center of the shop. "Running a little late this morning? You better hurry up, because if a customer comes in before you're ready, I'll dock your pay an hour."

"Understood."

"Understood what?"

She tossed her purse in the slot behind the counter and began her morning set up. "Understood, sir."

The side of his mouth quirked in a perverted, hungry grin. Mr. Watermore loved belittling her. It apparently turned him on, something she had the displeasure of realizing a few weeks ago. The memory of his closeness made her shiver.

"Don't forget to put the new sign out front."

Julia unfurled her fingers and snagged the sign. "Yes, sir." Her jaw snapped shut and her teeth clenched tight to keep her from unloading on him about his lazy, micromanaging, sexual-harassing attitude. He followed close behind her, too close. The scent of his cheap post-high-school-football-practice cologne made her nose run and her head throb in protest. She sniffled and walked faster; knowing Mr. Watermore wouldn't follow her out into the heat. Placing the sign safely out front, she took a moment to enjoy the fresh air.

Trianna passed in her old pickup and waved. Julia waved back, suddenly remembering she was supposed to call her last week about a girl's night out. She didn't have the time to go out, but still needed to remember to call her for a rain check.

Mr. Francisco, the owner of the Italian restaurant, pulled up, so she hurried inside to retrieve his order from the back. She made it to the counter just in time to greet him. "Good morning, Mr. Francisco. I have your order right here."

"Good Morning, Mrs. Cramer. It's a pleasure to see your smiling face. Everything's good, I trust?"

"Yes, the rack cards turned out perfect, but let's take a look together to make sure you're completely satisfied."

Mr. Watermore stepped out from his office. "Mr. Francisco is a busy man. I'm sure he doesn't have time right now."

Mr. Francisco waved his hand. "I always have time for Mrs. Cramer. You know, I remember when you and Mr. Cramer used to come to my restaurant for your anniversary. You always had little Ryan in tow and he would play with the dough the entire time you ate." He smiled. "He is good boy, just like you and his papa."

"Thank you. Ryan and I will have to find a time to come for dinner again." There was no way she could afford dinner there on her salary but that was no reason to be impolite.

"Yes. Yes. I look forward to it. Now, let us look at these." Mr. Francisco held out his hand and Julia unwrapped the rack cards and set them on the counter.

"Yes, yes. Perfecto. Thank you." Mr. Francisco paid for his order then leaned over the counter for his traditional kiss on both cheeks before he left.

Mr. Watermore, who'd watched the entire exchange with a snarl and that you-were-a-bad-girl stare, clicked his tongue. "Mrs. Cramer...Julia. We've spoken about this. Our guarantee on orders is only good until they exit the store. We do not encourage the customers to check their orders. If they ask, then you oblige, but otherwise we let them go."

She hated the way the man did business, and hated the fact there was nothing she could do about it. "You're the boss," she said with icy sweetness. "I'll make sure not to offer in the future."

Mr. Watermore moved toward her, so she turned to busy herself and stepped awkwardly with her right foot. Pain shot up her leg. She bent over in agony, noticing the side of her ankle was swollen. She could slip on the flats she always kept in her purse, but if she asked, he'd want to know why. And if she told him, he'd insist on looking at her ankle in mock concern. That involved his *innocent* touching.

He rounded the counter. "What is it? Did you hurt yourself?"

"I'm fine. Really," she said, straightening. "I should get back to work. You don't pay me to stand around doing nothing." Julia bit her bottom lip and stepped on her right foot again, making every effort not to limp.

"Here, sit down. Let me take a look." His hand grazed the small of her back, nudging her toward a chair, but she stiffened and sidestepped him.

"No, it's fine."

"I think I should take a look. After all, I don't want to be sued for you getting hurt at work."

Julia swallowed down the cry that clawed all the way from her ankle up her shins to her throat. "No need to worry. I just stumbled on the sidewalk in town. Now, if you'll excuse me." She turned to head the other way around the counter since he'd blocked the path to the back when the front door swung open and in rolled Maverick, with Ryan by his side.

Mr. Watermore rounded the counter. "What's your child doing here? We have an agreement."

"You also have an agreement not to sexually harass your employees." Maverick's words hung in the air, daring Mr. Watermore to fire her on the spot. One glance at the purple hue on his face told her she should brace herself for a lot of undignified groveling, right after she took Maverick to the top of the Appalachian Mountains and popped both his tires.

CHAPTER NINE

Maverick stared down Julia's boss, locked in a war of facial expressions. The stout man, his greasy skin glistening with sweat, fisted his hands at his sides. Maverick wheeled toward him, ready to fight for Julia's honor, but the man stumbled away.

The thought of him groping her fueled his desire to pummel the man into an early grave. If he was under Maverick's command, he could've taught the lowlife how to respect a beautiful woman, but here things were complicated. Civilian laws were lax.

Julia shuffled past Maverick, out of his line of sight. "Ryan, what are you doing here? You're supposed to be with Mr. Benjamin."

"I wanted to make sure you were okay."

Julia stepped between them. "And you?" She pointed one long, delicate finger at Maverick. "Tell me what you're doing here."

Maverick had no choice but to stand down. "Ryan wanted to see you, and we were driving by on the way to the site. James had to go in the opposite direction to drop Judy off at Cathy's so they could talk about the 4th of July event. Apparently, there's some sort of huge party happening." He knew he was babbling but couldn't help himself.

Julia's eyes narrowed, her beautiful full lips drawing thin. "It's more than just a party, but that's beside the point. I'll be talking to James. I entrusted my son to his care, not...not—"

Maverick lowered his head, unable to face her distrust of him. "I meant no harm."

She took two long breaths then leaned over, her hands braced on each armrest, her face only inches from his own. "Then take my son back to Mr. Benjamin."

He knew he should feel awful for whatever he'd done wrong, but all he could do was focus on her light floral scent and the fact her full lips were merely a breath away from his. She was adorable when she was angry. The way her eyes lit with fire. The way passion infused her voice. She was no woman to take orders from a man.

Ryan rushed at her. "Mama, it's not his fault. I told him you said it was okay that I was with him. You said this morning that I can't have a new dad, but I could have a big brother."

Julia rubbed her temples vigorously. "That's not what I said. Not what I meant, I mean." Her gaze darted around wildly, her breath quick and shallow. He'd seen that look before, the nervous twitch of her hands and the way she rubbed her head. It was how his men looked before battle. At that moment, he'd have done anything to ease her suffering.

"Hey, Ryan. It's okay. I'd love to be your big

brother, but your mom's right. I shouldn't have taken you without her permission, even if you did say it was okay. Please accept my apology."

"Mrs. Cramer," Mr. Watermore said sternly, "customers are arriving. I believe it would be best if your company left." His teeth clicked like a cicada at the end of each sentence.

"Yes, of course." Julia spun around, lost her footing, and grabbed onto the handle of his chair. He caught her, steadying her before she fell to the ground. She bent down and rubbed her right ankle. It looked larger than the other, red and puffy.

"You okay?"

"She's fine," Mr. Watermore snapped. "I was helping her to a chair when you showed up and started spouting unfounded accusations. You ex-military men are all alike, swooping in to help a damsel in distress just to feed your egos." Not brave enough to come around the counter and face Maverick like a man, he remained where he was and planted his hands on his hips. "Now, this is my business and I'd like you to leave."

He'd never wanted those darn prosthetic legs before now. The thought of towering over the smug S.O.B., intimidating him into watching his behavior around Julia, sounded like a good enough reason to strap those things on that instant. "As long as she welcomed your help. If not, I'd suggest you keep your hands to yourself. You wouldn't want to face a lawsuit for sexual harassment."

"That's enough," Julia snapped. "It's time for you

to go. Maverick, take my son to James. Ryan, you're to remain with Mr. Benjamin until I pick you up." She leaned over her son. "We'll talk about this tonight."

Her words stung more than a drill sergeant at boot camp. She didn't trust him with her son. But why should she? They'd just met. "Yes, ma'am. I'll head over there now."

Julia opened the door and stepped outside with them. She gave Ryan a hug and tweaked his nose before turning on Maverick. "Listen, I do appreciate your concern and your time with Ryan, but I can handle myself. I'm not in need of rescuing."

He opened his mouth to reply, but Mr. Watermore poked his head outside. "Mrs. Cramer, the phone is ringing. If you still work here, I suggest you answer it."

Rage boiled through him as he watched Julia scurry after the man. He didn't blame her. The pig had her in a tough spot. She needed the job to pay her bills and, from what Maverick understood, jobs were scarce in the area. If he had his way, he'd march her out of there and take care of her bills himself until her new veteran facility job began. But a woman like Julia was too proud to allow that kind of help.

"Come on, Ryan. Let's get you to the Benjamin farm."

Ryan shoved his hands in his pocket. "I'm sorry I got you in trouble."

Maverick opened the passenger door. "Don't worry about it, buddy. Trust me. I've been in worse scrapes."

He joined Ryan in the cab and headed toward the farm. "Your mother just wants what's best for you. I respect that. If I had kids, I'd want to protect them, too."

"If I had a dad, I wouldn't have to worry about my Mama so much."

He patted the little man on the shoulder. "You're doing a fine job. Your dad would be proud. Heck, I'm proud of you."

Ryan sat forward in the seat. "You are? How come?"

"Because you're brave and smart, and you love your mom. That makes you a good man."

Ryan quirked his head to the side. "Mr. Mav, why don't you have any kids? You'd make an awesome dad."

All the regret, remorse, and raw anguish he'd bottled up over the eight months crashed on top of him. He barely managed to keep his hands on the steering wheel and ignore the flashes of lost men and nightmares. After a minute of silence, he finally brandished an answer that he thought would appease the boy. "Because I'm not married."

"Why aren't you married?"

Kids were so inquisitive and honest. He remembered the children in the Zabul Province village he enjoyed working with during off hours. A few clicks in any direction meant trouble for US soldiers, but in this little village, they were sought out. The children soaked up everything the soldiers could teach them, from English and math, to making kickballs from bits of trash. Whenever he got a care package from Barbara, he'd always share his treasures with the children.

"Sorry," Ryan said. "I shouldn't ask. Mama says I

ask too many questions."

Maverick followed the winding road toward the Benjamin farm. "It's okay. You can ask me anything. I guess I'm not married because I haven't had time or met the right person." There. That should be good enough to hold off a kid. No need to get too deep.

Ryan adjusted his seatbelt away from his neck. "You have time now."

Maverick chuckled. "I don't know about that. I'll be busy with this new project for the next couple of months at least."

Ryan shook his head, his shaggy dark hair making him resemble a dog shaking off water. His father must've had dark hair and eyes, because Julia's were soft and pale, her strawberry-blond hair reminding him of a sunrise. "You have time at night. You only have one job."

He turned down the long drive to the farmhouse, ready to get out of the confined truck. "True, but it's still a busy one."

Ryan sighed. "My Mama works two jobs and still has time to have a date with me tonight. You could make time."

Maverick crested the hill and searched for James's car, but the yard out front was empty. Great. He wouldn't be able to escape the conversation after all. "That's different. You already have a mom. Finding a girl to date takes longer."

"So if you had a girl to date then you could get married?" Ryan asked.

"Sure, I guess so." Maverick stopped at the front of

the farmhouse and to his relief James's car came into view at the top of the hill.

Ryan hopped out of the truck and ran up to the front porch before Maverick managed to retrieve his chair and transfer into it.

Dark clouds were building in preparation for a late summer afternoon storm. Based on their angry color and mass, it would be a good one. Hopefully, it would lower the temperature to a bearable one.

"Thanks for bringing Ryan for me," James said as he climbed out of the car. "I'm surprised you're just getting here. I thought you guys would already be inside eating cookies."

"Nah, we made a stop on the way." He didn't want to talk about the disappointing reaction Julia Cramer had when he tried to help her.

Under James's watchful, judgmental eye, he maneuvered over the grass to the side ramp they'd installed. James waited at the top step, his gaze disapproving.

Maverick shook his head. "It's still easier than those darn prosthetic legs."

James held up his hands. "I didn't say a word. But now that you mention it, I spoke to the physical therapist at the VA. She said you need to go practice walking with your prosthetics. According to your records you skipped out of Miami before you completed your PT."

"What happened to patient confidentiality?" Maverick groaned.

"I didn't dig into your treatment, just your

appointments. That's allowed. Besides, I'm your doctor."

"No, you're not. I'm not paying you to shrink my head anymore, remember?"

James didn't say another word. He just turned and ruffled Ryan's hair before opening the front door of the pristine country home. "Did you stop for ice cream on the way here? If so, then I can't give you any cookies."

"No, we didn't have any sweets. We stopped to see Mama." Ryan rushed through the entryway, down the short hall to the kitchen. "So, I can have cookies."

James retrieved a container from the top of the refrigerator. "I thought you weren't supposed to go to her work."

Ryan hung his head. "I wasn't, but I don't like her boss."

James opened the Tupperware container and the room filled with the aroma of fresh baked treats. The home always smelled of something yummy, yet Judy and James managed to stay so thin from working the land.

"I see. You know, you shouldn't have disobeyed your mother, though." James set two cookies on the table in front of Ryan, but the boy's hands remained in his lap.

Guilt urged Maverick to confess. "It was my fault." He wheeled under the table and put a napkin on the table in front of him to wait for a cookie. "Ryan was uneasy after hearing about his mom's boss, so I took him by."

"I see," James said, holding his cookies ransom.

"You did it for Ryan? Not because you wanted to check on her yourself?"

"For Ryan." Maverick noticed his own hands remained in his lap.

"Hmm. Here, Ryan. You get an extra cookie for being a good son." James placed one more on the boy's napkin then closed the container.

"Hey, what about me?" Maverick's mouth was already watering at the thought of homemade cookies.

"You don't deserve one. You broke the rules."

He's kidding. Right?

Ryan bit into a cookie, but his wide eyes stayed fixed on James as the older man went to the refrigerator. "Want some milk?" he asked as he slid the container of cookies back on top of the refrigerator, out of reach.

Ryan nodded, his mouth still full of cookie.

Maverick gave James a playful glare. "Can I at least have something to drink?"

"Well, I don't know. Have you reflected on your actions?" As James took out three cups and filled each with milk, Ryan slid a cookie to Maverick.

He winked and shoved it in his mouth before James turned around, the cups of milk in hand.

Ryan took a sip. "Thank you."

James set a cup in front of Maverick, eying him. "It's polite to say thank you."

Maverick grabbed his glass and took a gulp to wash down the cookie. "Thank you."

James eyed them both suspiciously then sat down. "When you finish your cookies, why don't you go get the gardening bag from the barn and meet me out front. It's on the second shelf. I think you're tall enough to reach it."

Ryan downed his milk. "Yes, sir." He threw his napkin in the trash, rinsed his glass out, and then darted out the back door.

"He's such a good kid. He reminds me of a little boy I knew back in..." Maverick often wondered how the children of the village were doing. Where they were now and if the time they'd spent together had improved their lives at least a little.

"Back in Afghanistan?"

Maverick shrugged. "Yeah." If only... After his men were murdered, the village was abandoned. The people scattered, fearing the US would send drones to take out any remaining terrorists that had been hiding in their village.

"I'm sure he was special to you." James cleared the remaining glasses and put them in the dishwasher.

"They were all special." Maverick cleared his throat. Now wasn't the time to get lost in the past. He couldn't go back there, even just to visit in memories. It was still too real, too raw. So many soldiers had been killed, their loss haunting him in a waking nightmare.

A roll of thunder in the distance amplified his mood.

James opened the back door. "Guess we need to get to work before that storm blows in."

Maverick shook off the sadness and headed to the front ramp.

"Where you going?" James asked.

Maverick skidded to a halt and whirled around. "You getting senile? I can't go down the back steps. I'm headed for the ramp. I figured I'd help you guys get the gardening done then we could look over my proposed changes to the building plans."

"I'd love the help, but maybe next time. There won't be much you can do from your chair," James said, his words as light as a summer wind.

"I don't know what kind of trick you're working here, but I can help just fine. I'll just transfer to the ground."

"I'm sure that'd be fine, if we weren't going to garden on the other side of the creek bridge. We're starting a vegetable garden out there."

"I can manage. I've done more stairs than that. I'll just slide up on my butt. Nice try showing me that I can't do something without those legs, though."

Thunder sounded again, a little closer this time.

"Fine. We'll meet you out there." James shut the back door before Maverick could protest.

He turned back toward the front door. He'd show James his mind tricks wouldn't work on him. Didn't the man know who he was?

Without another thought, he wheeled down the ramp, out to the field and down the path toward the creek. Sticks crunched under his wheels and the chair bounced with the intensity of an 8.0 earthquake.

Halfway across the field, his arms and shoulders burned, but he wouldn't rest. He'd make James eat his words.

Heat lightening strobed across the sky and another

clap of thunder quickly followed, urging him to continue despite the fire in his back and gut. His biceps throbbed. He reached the steps and took several stuttered breaths. Sweat poured down his temples and back. At least he'd gotten a good workout. At this rate, he'd be able to skip the gym later. He eyed the ground and knew he had to dig deep to find the energy to transfer to the ground.

"You coming?" James called from the other side of the bridge.

He hadn't thought this through too well. He'd be forced to waddle over to the garden from the bridge, or drag his chair up the steps with him.

"Need some help?" James asked.

"No. I'm fine," Maverick hollered. He wasn't fine, though. He was exhausted and angry. Angry at James for baiting him into this, for asking him to prove the unreasonable. Fine. He'd manage somehow. He willed himself from the depths of exhaustion and transferred—no, flung himself onto the ground. His hip smacked against a rock and fiery pain shot up his back. "Ahhh."

"You okay?" Ryan yelled.

"Fine, bud," Maverick grunted under his breath. He rolled over and scooted his butt onto the first step, then the second, several minutes later he'd finally made it to the top of the bridge.

"You sure you don't need help?" Ryan asked.

Maverick looked up to find him hovering, with one eyebrow arched high on his head. Light broke through the clouds, shining over him like an angel in the darkness. "I'm fine. Go help Mr. B."

Ryan shrugged to his ears then spun around and ran off.

A drop of water hit Maverick on the nose. He looked up, more drops hitting him full in the face as it began to drizzle.

James appeared at his side. "Looks like we should head back to the house. Rain's coming. Besides, we got the area cleared for the fall garden. It wasn't as much work as I thought."

Maverick gritted his teeth like a pit bull at the start of a dogfight. "Really?" He looked up at James, squinting against the raindrops.

"What?" The old man had the nerve to stand there with a slack mouth and wide eyes. Hell no. He wasn't getting away with this.

"You did this on purpose to make a point. I wheeled all the way across that field from the house. Over rocks, sticks, holes big enough to bury a dead body, not to mention the bugs that are burrowing into my gums as we speak."

"Why'd you wheel all the way up here? I thought you'd bring your truck to the bridge."

Maverick swung his head around to the truck sitting in the front lawn. "You...I... Ahh!"

"Always trying to prove you know what's best doesn't mean you really do. By the way, you have a flat tire."

CHAPTER TEN

Daylight still shone in the sky, but her body screamed it had to be well past midnight. Julia turned onto the Benjamins' drive, happy to finally be picking up Ryan. The day had dragged on forever, with Mr. Watermore's silent treatment making the tension in the shop higher than usual. At first, it was a pleasant change, but each time he passed, she waited for him to announce she was fired. If only she could quit. The constant threat of losing her job was taking its toll.

On top of that, she still felt guilty for treating Ryan so harshly earlier, not to mention Maverick. He was in the wrong for butting in, but Henry would've done no less. She couldn't do anything to make it up to Maverick, but she could treat Ryan to an amazing night.

As she crested the hill, Maverick's truck came into view. Did the man ever go home? She hobbled from the car to the front porch, shielding her head from the pelting rain, each step shot pain up her right calf. Darn ankle had swollen even more throughout the day. Even the comfortable flats she'd switched into didn't feel any better.

The front door swung open and Ryan leapt into her arms. "I'm so glad you're here. I was worried." His arms were tight around her waist and his body shook.

She glanced at her watch. "I'm right on time, honey. What's wrong?"

Ryan shook his head. "Nothin', Mama. I just missed you. And it's raining outside and you were driving."

She peeled him from her body, but noticed the fright in his eyes. It broke her heart to see him so shaken. "I missed you, too, but I'm here now."

He took her hand and pulled her inside the house. "Best get inside before the lightening gets close again."

Since when was Ryan scared of storms?

She followed him into the living room. The aroma of fresh brewed coffee filled the room and her mood lifted a bit. A steaming cup of coffee was just what she needed.

James and Maverick were talking in the kitchen so she sat on the edge of the couch to steal a moment with her son before she thanked them for watching him. "Hold up a second, I want to tell you something before we go see Mr. Benjamin." The couch cushion sunk deep and she was tempted to snuggle into one of the oversized pillows and fall fast asleep. "I wanted to apologize for earlier. You were so sweet to come check on me. It's just that I'm trying hard to hang onto that job right now. I've finally dug us out of debt, and I don't want to go back to charging things again. It's just me and you now, so we need to work together."

"But I don't want that man hurting you." Ryan

crossed his arms over his chest, his angry brow looking out of place on her little man.

"You know what? Your daddy taught me how to take care of myself."

"He did?" Ryan's pupils swelled.

"Yes, before he left for basic training. He wanted to make sure I could protect myself while he was away. I tell you what. I promise that if Mr. Watermore ever does anything I think is over the line, I'll pull one of those moves your daddy taught me. He'll have more than just a busted lip when I'm done with him."

Ryan smirked. "I know this isn't right, but I'd like to see that. I think I'd like to do that myself."

Julia couldn't help but laugh. "I know, son, but violence is a last resort. I'd only do it if I didn't have any other options."

"Wise woman," James said from the doorway. "Hey, you weren't leaving without helping me upstairs first, were you? You promised to help me put up that shelf."

"Oh, that's right. Is it okay, Mama? Do you mind?" Ryan hopped between his feet, that I-get-to-do-man-things grin on his face.

"It's fine, but don't take too long. Tonight's your night, remember? We'll do whatever you want."

"Awesome." Ryan darted upstairs; James climbed the stairs in his wake.

Julia followed the aroma of coffee to the kitchen. "I smell fresh coffee. Do you mind if I grab a cup? I could use a little pick-me-up."

"Of course. Help yourself," James replied from the

top of the stairs.

She pushed through the swinging door into the kitchen and spotted Maverick. Maverick, with his shirt off.

The way he faced away from her, arm muscles active and posed, she thought he was a marble figure of the man her son had taken to. Because no living being could have a body like that. Lines of defined muscle swooped in all directions from his shoulders, drawing her eye down his back to his waistline.

Julia clasped the side of the sink to keep herself up right, the air in her lungs evaporating like droplets of water on asphalt in the middle of July.

He moved, each muscle rippling in response, but the image of perfection didn't fade. Only airbrushed models looked like that. She blinked a few times, but the illusion remained. The way he sat, he looked unharmed. A man with no war wounds or lost limbs.

"You going to continue gawking, or are you going to help?"

A gasp shot from her mouth.

He spun around. "Oh, I thought you were James."

She'd always prided herself on being cool-headed. Not much fazed her. But when he turned, his chest expanding and contracting at a quick pace, she'd lost all thought and words.

"You okay? That monster didn't—"

"No." She shook her head. "I didn't know you were in here. You startled me. That's all."

He pushed a chair out. "Here. Have a seat. I'm just repairing my wheel."

She didn't move. She couldn't imagine being that close to him and not touching his body to see if it was real. He lowered his chin to his chest then grabbed his shirt, a dusting of pink flushing his cheeks. That boyish blush touched her soul while her eyes feasted on one last glimpse of his muscles before he yanked the shirt over his head.

"Sorry. James just brought my shirt back from the dryer. I got stuck in the rain earlier when my tire blew out."

What was wrong with her? Maverick was just another hero waiting to save the day then disappear out of her life. The same way her brother, father, and husband had. No, she was done with that type of man.

Julia grabbed a mug. "Do you want some coffee?"

"No." He held up a hand then went back to his tire. "I'd be up all night if I drank any this late."

"Exactly. I'm hoping it keeps me awake for at least a few hours. I don't want to disappoint Ryan. He's had enough of that lately."

Maverick set his tools aside. "He's a good kid. I hate to hear he's had a rough time. He's the reason I took this project on. It's hard to disappoint the kid."

Julia poured coffee into her mug, added cream then sat across the table from Maverick. He was a good-looking man, but she'd seen others. It was just the shock of seeing him shirtless. She was a widow, a mother, a hard worker, but she was still a woman. And no woman could have ignored that display.

"Ryan has a way with people. Just like his father." There. Bringing up her husband would let him know he didn't affect her, despite her momentary lapse in sanity.

Maverick leaned over, catching her gaze in his. Only then did she realize she'd been staring at his chest. Heat raced over her skin. She lifted her mug to hide behind it, wishing it was the size of a barrel.

When she lowered the cup to the table, she caught his smug smile.

Maverick clasped his hands together on the table in front of him. "So, what ya doing on your big date tonight?"

"Whatever Ryan wants. I told him it was his choice. I felt bad about snipping at you guys earlier. Even though you shouldn't have been there, I still didn't need to lose my temper."

Maverick spun his wheel resting on its side on the table. "Yeah, well, I guess I over-stepped. I can do that sometimes. I'm sorry. I'll respect your wishes in the future."

Future? Her heart did a cha-cha on her ribs. "I'd appreciate that. I won't get so mad next time, either. Deal?"

Maverick held out a hand. "Deal."

Her insides spun in anticipation. The thought of touching him, even if it was just his hand, frightened her. Not of him, but of herself. If he affected her this much from merely looking, what would touching do? But what choice did she have? She couldn't leave him hanging. She took his hand. Gentle grasp, soft, strong, amazing. More than she'd feared and hoped from a single touch. She ignored the tympanic march in her neck, the way a pleasant sensation dance on her skin. She ignored the air swooshing from her lungs. But she couldn't ignore the crisp, grey eyes that welcomed her into his world.

"Mama? Mama. You ready to go?"

A smidgen of disappointment pecked at her resolve, but she pulled her hand from his and stood. "Yes. Let's go."

"Wait." Ryan hopped up onto Maverick's lap. "You're coming, too."

Maverick shot a sideways glance at Julia. "That's nice of you, but I don't want to interrupt your date with your mom. That's too special. Men would be falling all over themselves to be in your shoes."

Men? Falling all over themselves? Would he?

"Mama's special, but we can share her. I don't mind. We'll grab pizza and hang out at home. We're gonna have a picnic in our living room. It'll be fun. Don't say no. Pleeeaase?"

Maverick's gaze darted around the kitchen as if hunting for the correct answer.

Julia decided to save him. "Listen, maybe another night. I'm sure Maverick already has plans."

"That's right. I told James we'd go over the blueprints for the project. That's too important to miss."

James poked his head through the doorway. "Nope, not tonight. I've got a hot date of my own. Lisa's planning meeting let out early, so I'm meeting Judy at Francisco's for a nice romantic dinner. We'll get together tomorrow."

Maverick scooted Ryan off his lap, retrieved the wheel, and placed it atop his chair lying sideways on the floor. "Even so, I'm sure your mother would prefer it be the two of you."

"She said I could do whatever I want," Ryan said. "Invite whoever I want. I want to eat pizza and invite you."

Julia couldn't sit back and let her son railroad the poor man into eating with them. "I said I would do anything with *you*. You can't bully Mr. Maverick into eating with us tonight."

Ryan kicked an imaginary pebble across the kitchen floor. "Yes, ma'am."

"Oh, he doesn't mind," James said. "Besides, he doesn't cook and he's usually up for anything. Right, Maverick?" James winked before retreating out the kitchen door.

A strange expression swept over Maverick's face, a wrinkled brow, pressed lip kind of expression.

Julia needed to end this and get Ryan out of the kitchen before any more awkwardness could ensue. "Listen, Ryan—"

"I'll buy the pizza."

Julia smacked her lips. "What?"

Maverick screwed the bolt back through his wheel. "I said I'd buy the pizza. It's my way of saying sorry for almost getting you fired. Even if the boss man deserves to be slapped with a lawsuit."

"You don't have to buy pizza. I've already accepted your apology." Julia needed to get out of this. She hadn't had a man in her home since she lost Henry. It felt wrong to bring another man into the home they'd bought together. The home they'd raised their child in.

Maverick turned his chair upright and scooted into the seat. "It's my pleasure. Just tell me where, when, and what type of pizza."

"Now. Our house. Pepperoni and sausage," Ryan cried cheerfully, sliding his hand into his mother's. "Let's go. We'll rent a movie."

"Ryan, I—"

"I'll see you there," Maverick said, cutting her off. His words hung in the air, a silence growing between them until Ryan dragged her out of the kitchen, out of the house, and out of her comfort zone. What just happened? She was having a man over? A man with silver eyes, a chiseled jaw, soft hands, and a body only Michelangelo could have created. A man who she knew could turn her inside out if she let him.

No. He was a hero, and not her husband. She lowered her head in shame. How could she even think of another man? Henry had only died a year ago. It was too soon. Even this lifetime was too soon.

CHAPTER ELEVEN

Maverick pulled into the small driveway of three twenty-five Knoll Road. A small, cottage-style home, with wilting flowers in window boxes, a bent screen in the right front window, cracked cobblestone walkway, and a lot of weeds.

He parked behind Julia's green Oldsmobile, his wheels half off the two strips of concrete, barely visible through the overgrowth.

The peeling paint and broken gutter on the right corner of the roof screamed for attention. If only he could climb a ladder to fix it for her.

He transferred to his chair, maneuvered over the rocky overgrowth, and opened the passenger door to the battling scents of pepperoni and perennials. The florist near the pizza shop had drawn him in with the echo of his mother's words in his head. *Never show up without a hostess gift when going to someone's home.* He'd always followed that rule, but flowers? What possessed him to think that was a good idea?

A pounding sound drew his attention to the front window. Ryan waved madly, his smiling face illuminated by a dim light behind him.

Maverick grabbed the flowers and placed them on top of the pizza on his lap then slammed the door. The heat from the pizza penetrated his shorts, but he had no choice. He had to leave the box on his lap while he wheeled to the front door. A ceramic gnome mocked him from the sticks and sun-damaged bushes in the front garden, with his you're-a-sucker expression.

Ryan flung the door open before Maverick had a chance to toss the flowers into the bushes. "Come in!"

Maverick propped his front wheels up then rolled over the step and into Julia Cramer's home. Ryan took the pizza with flowers still on top from his lap and carried it into the dining room, as Maverick rubbed the sting from his quads.

The home was small, but unlike the neglected exterior, the inside was perfect, not a pillow out of place in the living room to his right, and not a speck of dust on the entry table.

Ryan returned the flowers to him. "I'll let you give these to my Mama yourself. She loves flowers. Used to pick them from the garden when we had time to plant them."

Maverick followed Ryan down the hall, ignoring the pattering of his pulse against his skin.

"Mama also likes dancing. Can you dance? I saw a girl in a wheelchair dance on a video once, but I heard James say you have legs. So does that mean you can dance? Why don't you use your legs?"

"Ryan, stop badgering our guest and let him come inside," Julia called from the kitchen. The soft jazz floating down the hall made him want to dance. He'd never had the desire to walk on those darn legs before, let alone dance.

"I didn't know what flavor you liked, so I bought a couple extra cupcakes."

Maverick turned the corner to find Julia wearing a summer dress. Not just any summer dress, one that fit her waist, the little tie in the middle accentuating her chest. Her usual suits and heels had nothing on her standing in the kitchen bare foot with pink toenails in a hip-hugging dress. At that moment, he was glad Mr. Watermore demanded she wear business attire. Because no man would be able to take their eyes off her in that outfit.

Julia removed a cupcake from the box, and licked the frosting from her slender finger. "I didn't even know if you ate cupcakes. A man with your body... Uh, I mean, it's obvious you take care of yourself. I—"

"I love cupcakes. Not choosy on the flavor," he said to rescue her, although he liked seeing her blush. The warm tone accentuated her high cheekbones.

She smiled, one that would convince a man to dive onto a live grenade if she asked. Julia rounded the counter and took the flowers from him. "They smell beautiful. I haven't had flowers in my kitchen since..." A sadness crossed her face and he wished he could stand. Stand and pull her into his arms to relieve her grief. He knew how lonely she had to be raising a child on her own. She deserved to be happy.

"I'll put them in water." She turned, the hem of her dress lifting as she spun. But the pale-green material fell too soon, framing her body once more.

She filled the vase with water, cut the stems, and placed the arrangement in the center of the kitchen table. His mother was right. He should never show up to a person's house empty-handed. The way Julia straightened the flowers with an admiring gaze made him want to go kick that mocking gnome from her garden.

"You ready to watch the movie?" Ryan called, racing into the kitchen. "Mama said we can even eat in the living room while we watch. She put a blanket down and lots of pillows. This is going to be so much fun!" He disappeared around the corner without waiting for a reply.

Julia snagged the plate of cupcakes. "You regret accepting his invitation yet?"

"Not in the least." Maverick spun his chair around and went back the way he'd come, figuring the other doorway wasn't large enough for him to fit his chair through. This home wouldn't be up on ADA specifications. Something he needed to consider in the changes to the outer buildings at the veteran facility.

She stopped at the edge of the blanket. "Um...will you be okay. I mean, you know, getting onto the floor?"

Maverick rolled past her, lifted the arm of the chair, and lowered to the floor. "Does that answer your question?"

"I'm sorry. I didn't mean to—"

Maverick opened a pizza box that Ryan had placed in the center of the blanket. "No need. You don't know me any more than I know you. I'm just glad you're not allergic to flowers. You're not, are you?"

Julia lowered gracefully to the only remaining spot on the blanket. Her dress floated for a moment then landed around her legs. "I'm not." She sat so close their legs would be touching if he still had his. She smelled fresh, like a blooming flower. Not the pungent kind, but a light fragrance that drew you to sniff the bud. He thought of the color purple, like a lilac.

The TV clicked on, blaring some news report involving a political scandal. Ryan changed the input to DVD and hit *play.*

Julia whispered, "I hope an action film is okay." Her warm breath breezed across his ear lope.

Hair on the back of his neck stood at attention. "It's fine," he whispered back. "I'm not one of those vets who'll dive under the table at the first sound of gun fire. Not that a real gunshot wouldn't cause me to react."

Julia nodded then retrieved a piece of pizza, taking her warm breath and soothing scent with her.

Ryan sat cross-legged, his eyes super-glued to the television. "Mama let me get this. She usually won't let me watch anything with a language warning, but I promised I wouldn't repeat no words."

"Any words," Julia corrected.

Ryan didn't respond—they'd already lost him to the first preview.

"We usually stick with G-rated films," she explained. "This is his first action flick. I hope it doesn't give him nightmares."

Ryan devoured his pizza without taking his gaze from the screen.

Maverick smiled. "I think he'll be fine."

Three more previews rolled while they sat in silence, eating. Then *Mission Impossible*, with Tom Cruise, started and Maverick relaxed. He was always spouting about not being affected by the war, but the death grip he had on his soda can told him that wasn't exactly accurate.

Julia finished her piece and cleared the plates and pizza. "Be right back. I'm afraid my OCD won't allow me to leave dirty dishes on the floor."

Ah, that explained the interior of the house, Maverick thought.

She walked away, favoring one foot. When she returned and rubbed her right ankle, he asked, "You okay?"

Julia gave a short huff. "Yes, I'm just a Klutz. A klutz that should never wear heals. I took on a curb in town today and the curb won. It's no big deal. I just twisted it."

"You want me to take a look. I might not be a doctor, but I have plenty of field experience."

"No, it's fine. I don't want to trouble you."

"It's no trouble. Really."

Ryan held a finger to his lips. "Shh!"

"Sorry." Julia gave him an apologetic smile. "I'm afraid he's a little excited about this movie."

Maverick turned so one stump crossed his body and the other one pointed out to the side. "Here. Put your foot on my leg or I'll keep talking. And we wouldn't want to interrupt his movie."

Julia toyed with the hem of her dress for a moment, then sheepishly glanced his way before rotating to face him. She tucked her dress around her thighs and placed one perfect foot on his leg. Her foot was attached to a firm, long leg that was silky to the touch. And he liked touching it.

"It's a little swollen. Have you iced it?" Maverick asked.

"For a few minutes. I haven't had any more time to spare than that. I'll ice it again." Julia placed her hands on the floor to move away, but he kept hold of her foot.

"Wait. Let me just make sure nothing's broken." He ran his fingers up each of her metatarsals. Nothing indicated a break, but she did stiffen under his touch. Was it from pain, or did she not like his hands on her? When she didn't pull away, he continued massaging up the side of her foot to her ankle. She relaxed and closed her eyes.

The softness of her skin, like a satiny feather, one you wanted to hold between your fingers all day, drew him closer. His heart swelled with a long, lost hope. The hope of living again.

Ryan squealed, shattering their moment. Julia slipped her foot from his hands. "Thank you. It's much better now."

Some action sequence roared to life onscreen and they both turned. But Maverick didn't keep his eyes on the TV for long. His gaze drifted back to Julia's thin frame. Nothing in the movie could entertain him more than to watch her sit on her side and run her hand through her hair. How long had it been since he was this close to a beautiful woman. A year? More? Even after he'd returned from war, Barbara only came to the hospital a few times, but she always kept her distance. She never wanted to look at him, let alone touch him.

Throughout the remainder of the movie, his attention caught at key points, but most of the time he kept it on Julia and her graceful movements. When the credits began to roll, he looked over to find Ryan fast asleep on the floor. "Poor guy didn't even get his cupcake."

Julia crawled to Ryan's side and slid her arms underneath him. "He never makes it through a movie, but he loves them. And don't worry. He'll get his cupcake in the morning. I'll make an exception for breakfast since it's Saturday." She lifted him into her arms.

"Do you need some help?" he offered.

That awkward, one lifted eyebrow expression showed on her face. "That's okay. It's upstairs."

"Don't worry about it. I should be going anyway." Maverick grabbed the edge of his wheelchair seat and tugged it toward him.

"No. Wait. I mean, we still have all those cupcakes to eat." Her cheeks flushed ever so slightly, a light delicate sweep of color. "You'd be doing me a favor. I don't want them left here alone with me. I'm likely to gain twenty pounds by morning."

"You'd still look beautiful." The words flew from his lips before he could steel-trap them. What was wrong with him tonight? You'd think he'd never seen a pretty girl before.

Julia shifted Ryan between her arms. "Thank you. It's been a long time since someone's said that to me."

Maverick pushed his chair out of the way and scooted to the couch. "I'd love a cupcake."

She smiled shyly before disappearing upstairs. The room fell quiet except for the occasional creak of the floorboards upstairs. Yet, it was welcoming with the smell of pizza, cupcakes, and an aroma he couldn't quite place. A kind of at-home fragrance. He pulled himself up onto the couch and eyed his missing legs. For several months after the accident, he had phantom pain and itching, but now he'd adjusted to the point of it being normal to have to crawl up and over things.

Maybe tomorrow he should dust off those fake legs and give them a try. But did he deserve to walk when his men were still dead in the ground? What gave him the right to live on?

"Does it still hurt?" Julia stood on the bottom step, her head tilted enough for stray hair to fall over her face in a way that made her even more beautiful. She pointed at his leg, where he'd been absently rubbing his right stump.

"No. Not anymore."

"That's good." She twirled the end of the stray piece of hair around her finger and bit her bottom lip. The little movement stole any remaining doubt and locked him in her world, with no hope of parole.

Moving across the room, Julia placed her hand over his and squeezed. "You might not know it, but you're lucky."

Maverick shrugged. "I guess."

"It must've been tough, when you realized you'd lost your legs. But you seem to be doing well."

"I'm fine. As you said, I was the lucky one."

Her hand slipped away. "I'm sorry. I didn't mean to pry. I guess we know where Ryan gets his curious nature from."

"I like Ryan's curiosity. I don't mind questions, or people looking at my injury." He hiked his shorts up above his stumps. Heck, you can touch it if you want." *Touch it?* What the hell was he saying? He didn't even like to touch the blasted scars.

She traced a scar line from the center to the jagged edges. He saw her fingers, but couldn't feel them, not physically. But his neurons rapid-fired at the thought of her analyzing his tragedy. Her finger slid to the end of the scar. A light touch, so light it caused his skin to prickle and his breath to short circuit.

"Sorry. Did I hurt you?"

Maverick shook his head, the words trapped in his constricting throat.

She moved her hand to the other side and followed another line to the center. By the time she reached the middle he thought he'd collapse from lack of oxygen. His pulse beat as hard as a morning run in full gear, fifty pound pack and all. "It's like diamonds."

"Huh?" Maverick managed between labored breaths.

"The shape of your scars. They look like you have a diamond on the end of each leg." She turned, leaving his body, mind, and soul in a firefight of will. Did he hold her hand? Did he lean into her? Did he stay far away? He wanted to scream *Mayday* before he imploded with uncertainty.

Before he could decide, she snagged two of the cupcakes and handed him one. "Bon appetit."

He took the cupcake, if for no other reason than to have something to keep his hands busy before he did something stupid like tried to kiss her. The vanilla and cinnamon exploded in his mouth with delicious intensity. "Wow. This is amazing."

"Yeah, the Cupcake Lady, Karen Wanke, is the most amazing baker. I'm surprised you haven't had something made by her yet. She usually drops off samples and donations all over Creekside. You'll probably get to meet her at the new facility. She tends to cater things for veterans and other groups." A speck of chocolate frosting took up residence on the edge of her lip and he would have done anything to taste it. Apparently, civilian life stole his discipline. That had to change and quick.

"You've got a little..."

She snagged a napkin and dabbed her lips, but it remained. Discipline faded to desire and he wiped it with his thumb from the corner of her lips. When her tongue darted out at the same time and caught the edge of his finger, he felt like he should drop and give twenty push-ups for his body's reaction.

"Thanks." She finished the rest of her cake and cleaned up immediately. "Sorry. I know, I can't help but clean if there's anything out of place. Guess you should know my faults before you agree to let me work at the facility."

"You're talking to an ex-military man. Cleaning is sexy." When she rounded the corner to the kitchen, he smacked his forehead. "Get a grip," he whispered to himself.

"I'm getting excited about this project," she called. "At first, I thought it was insane, but now... I don't know. It's like we can give back and move forward all at the same time." She returned and sat by his side, right by his side. "That probably makes no sense."

"Makes perfect sense." Maverick knew the importance of such a project, but despite James essentially tricking him into it, he hadn't kicked and screamed too much. He may not feel he deserved any redemption but this was still a chance to give a little bit to those families that lost loved ones. Loved ones like the ones he'd left widowed.

"You okay? That dark shadow passed over your face again."

"Dark shadow?" Maverick asked.

"Something my mother would say when someone faced a bad memory."

"Your mother's wise."

"Was. She died years ago."

"I'm sorry."

She tucked stray hair behind her ear. "Ryan's all I have now, but he fills the void well."

Maverick squeezed her hand this time. "He's an amazing boy. You're doing a great job raising him." He could feel her hand tremble before she slipped it away and grabbed the remote.

"I hope so. I worry that he needs a father figure." She shifted and fumbled her thumb over the buttons. "I'm not saying—"

Maverick held up a hand. "Don't worry. You don't strike me as a husband-finding kind of girl. You're way too independent."

She laughed. "You mean I nearly take a guy's head off for trying to defend my honor?" The laugh wasn't high-pitched or shrill, just. It was soft and soothing like her voice, skin, and soul.

"Yeah, there's that."

She smacked him with the remote. "Hey."

Maverick scooted back on the couch, rubbing his arm where she'd smacked him in mock pain. "You said it," he replied with a shrug.

Her laugh faded to a chuckle but the smile on her face remained bright. "You want to watch a little TV? I can't believe I'm saying this, but I'm not tired and wouldn't mind some adult company. I love my son, but it's nice to have a conversation that doesn't center around a cartoon character."

"Sure. I don't have anything going on tonight. I just need to meet James at the site tomorrow at oh-seven-hundred-hours to go over my proposed changes to the original plans. We want to get started Monday morning on the work."

She pressed a button and the TV switched to cable, a scene from the old movie *Logan's Run* lighting up the screen. "Ah, I love this movie."

"Me, too. I've always enjoyed watching old films." Maverick braced his arm against the back of the couch and scooted into the corner to get comfortable.

She slouched and propped her feet on the coffee table. His arm trapped behind her. Light flickered in the dark room from the screen, but his body remained frozen, his mind not comprehending anything about the film. All of his senses were filled with her.

"I love this part—when he realizes it's all a farce." She snuggled into the pillows and his hand touched her shoulder.

There was a time when he knew exactly how to win a girl over; when he could have any woman he wanted without even trying. But now? Now, things were different. He hadn't even touched a woman for nearly a year.

After ten minutes or so, Julia's head started to bob. She scooted lower and rested her head on his shoulder. A few breaths later, he held her in his arms while she slept and he'd never been happier. But did he have the right? Didn't he deserve to be miserable for the rest of his days?

CHAPTER TWELVE

"**M**ama, you had a sleepover!" Ryan's words penetrated Julia's haze and she slowly opened her eyes.

"What, honey?" She lifted her head and realized her body was wrapped in warm, strong arms. His arms. *Oh my God. I fell asleep on him?*

The world came into view, with bright sunlight flooding into the room. Their picnic blanket remained on the floor, and there on the couch was Maverick, by her side, holding her all night.

He stirred to life, wiping his eyes. "Hey, little man," he said, his deep, sexy voice warming her insides.

"You had a sleepover with Mama. She never lets me have one," Ryan huffed and crossed his arms.

"We didn't have a sleepover." She sat up and willed her brain to focus. To somehow explain this situation to her son. But how, when she couldn't even explain it to herself?

Ryan huffed. "You slept. It's morning. That's a sleepover."

She looked to Maverick and whispered, "Help."

"He has a point," he murmured. "You fell asleep next to me, and it is morning." He winked—a playful, I'm-hot-and-I-know-it wink.

It was too early, and she needed coffee before she could properly deal with this. "Fine, but it wasn't meant to be a sleepover. Mama was tired from working and she fell asleep watching a movie. Mr. Maverick must've fallen asleep, too." She looked at Maverick. The man she'd slept next to last night. A man that wasn't her husband. Guilt pounded at her like a printing press, smashing in thoughts of betrayal repeatedly until it was stamped on her heart.

She stood up a bit too quickly and teetered.

"Hey, you okay?" Maverick touched her upper arm, only a light sentiment but the ink mark on her heart faded to bearable.

She nodded. "I'll get you some breakfast. Want coffee?"

"I'd love some," he said. But before she could even limp to the kitchen, he was in his wheelchair and rolling through the other doorway. He snagged the coffee pot and began filling it with water.

"Oh, no! It's already seven-thirty. Don't you need to meet James?"

Maverick slid his phone from his pocket and swiped the screen. "Nope. Looks like he changed it to oh-nine-hundred. I have time." Pouring the water into the coffee maker, he said, "Hey, I was thinking. You don't have to work today, right?"

She pulled out a frying pan then retrieved some eggs from the fridge. "No. Saturday's the one day I spend with Ryan. That and Sunday morning."

He placed the coffee pot in the unit and flicked the switch on. "Would you two like to go to the site with me? I'd love the input of our future organizer."

She tossed some butter in the frying pan. "I don't mind but it's up to Ryan. I don't want him to be bored on our only day together."

"I won't be bored. Promise. I want to go." Ryan opened the drawer, took out some forks, and then moved the stepstool over to the cabinet to retrieve plates and mugs.

Eggs sizzled and the rich aroma of coffee filled the room. "I guess we're going then. I just need to change and freshen up first. I won't be long."

"We have time. Besides, doesn't someone get a cupcake after breakfast?"

Ryan hopped off the stool, his eyes wide with anticipation. "Can I?"

She nodded and he took off to retrieve it from the living room.

Alone with Maverick, her hand trembled and she gripped the spatula tighter. "I can't believe I fell asleep with food left on the table. I must've been exhausted. I usually can't sleep until everything is put in its place."

"I know what you mean. My drill sergeant ruined me for life. I was flipped out of my bunk once too many times during basic training that I never forget to tidy up before I go to sleep. I went into the military a slob and came out a neat freak." Maverick swiveled around the kitchen like he belonged there, and she liked it. "Hey, you're still favoring that ankle. I want to wrap it before you do any major walking today. Do you have a bandage?"

The thought of him touching her foot again heated her flesh. "I'll be fine."

"Still, I'd feel better if I at least took another look. If you don't have a bandage, I'm sure James has some. We can wrap it when we get to his place."

"That's not necessary. I have some if we need it." She set the plates on the table and Ryan dashed to the kitchen table. "Oh, I forgot. I need to pick up my work for tomorrow night from Cathy."

Maverick poured a cup of coffee and handed it to her. His fingers grazed her knuckles and she imagined what it would be like to walk hand and hand with him.

It was strange to look down at a man. Her husband was several inches taller than her. Based on Maverick's frame, she'd guessed he would've easily been six feet or taller. What was even stranger was that his lack of height didn't make him seem any less manly.

She carried the frying pan to the table and slid a fried egg onto each plate. Before sitting down, she cupped Ryan's face. He had icing smeared across his cheeks. "Eat up, munchkin. I don't want to be late to meet Ms. Cathy. And eat a few bites of protein or you'll be flying around the room until you crash and burn."

"Yes, ma'am," Ryan grumbled despite the huge bite of cake in his mouth.

Maverick and Ryan chatted happily as they ate while Julia sipped her coffee, listening to their banter. The morning was full. Her home was full and her heart was full. But was this right? *Henry, am I betraying you? Would you want Ryan and me to have a new family without you?*

Maverick nudged her arm. "You okay?"

Julia inhaled the stale smell of confusion. "Just thinking."

Maverick scooped the last bit of egg into his mouth then cleared his plate and took Ryan's. "Why don't you go brush those teeth, little man, and we'll head out?"

Ryan took the last swig of milk. "Can we ride in your truck?"

"If that's okay with your mom."

"Um, sure." She shook the haze from her head. "Wait. That would mean you'd have to drive us home again. I don't want to put you out."

"You're not. I have to come back into town to meet a man about delivering the last bit of supplies to the site Monday morning anyway."

"Woohoo!" Ryan yelled as he thundered up the stairs.

Quiet saturated the room. Maverick scooted in next to her and took her hand. "Listen, I know you've been through a lot. So have I. There hasn't been a moment that I've even thought about a woman since I was discharged from the hospital. I struggled just to breathe the first few weeks, then to move, and to live. If what I've been doing is even living." He gave her a weak smile. "According to James, I've only been surviving. The point is, there doesn't have to be anything between us. We can be friends, partners on this project. I don't want to create any more stress in your life. It's obvious that you loved your husband, and based on that little

107

angel you've got, he was a good man. He had to be to have you as his wife." He sighed but squeezed her hand a little tighter. "I'm not great with words, but I wanted to let you know I expect nothing from you. I just want to offer my help anyway I can."

She couldn't think, not with his hands on hers. The warmth of his touch twisted her brain, squeezing the thoughts from her head. Not even her lungs received the message that she should breathe. Maverick Wilson, a gorgeous, sensitive, amazing man that loved her son, sat by her side holding her hands. *God, what do I do? Henry, what would you want?*

Maverick slid his hands from hers, but she grabbed them and held them tight. "No." Her bottom lip quivered and she fought to control her shaking voice. "I don't want you to replace Henry. No one could replace him."

He nodded, but she knew he didn't understand. She wouldn't release his hands, wouldn't release his promise, she wouldn't release him. "But..." Tears swelled in her eyes and she tried to blink them away. Her entire body shook and his face filled with concern.

"But what?" His hand tugged free and his thumb brushed tears from her cheeks. "Talk to me. Tell me what I can do."

"I don't know. I'm struggling and... I know you can't replace Henry. I've got to figure things out, but all I know is that I don't want you to go. There's something here, something I haven't felt in a long time. Something I thought I'd never feel again. I don't know if it's just loneliness, having a person to fill the emptiness in my life, or if I really like you." She couldn't believe what she was saying, but she had to make him understand. "My heart's not ready to know for sure. My first thought when I woke in your arms wasn't of Henry and that scared me. There's never been anyone but Henry since I was a teenager and I don't know how to feel about that." She brought her gaze up to meet his. "I can't promise anything, except that I want you around. I understand if that's not enough."

He cupped her cheek. "It's everything. It's all I ask."

She rested her forehead against his, breathed his air, felt his touch, embraced the moment.

Hearing footsteps rumble down the stairs, she pulled away before she was ready, wiped her tears, and busied herself with straightening the few remaining things out of place in the kitchen.

"Hey, little man," Maverick said.

Ryan burst into the kitchen. "You ready to go?"

The emotion she could hear in his voice brought on a fresh wave of tears and she fought to keep them from spilling over. She'd kept so much bottled inside for so long, to be strong for Ryan. Why here? Why now? Life never happened the way she'd planned, but she knew it was time to make some changes, if for no other reason than for Ryan. No, for herself. "I'll be right back. I need to change."

As she fled the kitchen, Maverick put Ryan on his lap and twirled him around on his chair. Ryan's giggles filled the house. She'd tried so hard to give everything he needed, but when was the last time he'd laughed like that?

The third step, the one Henry had fixed right after they'd moved in, creaked underfoot. Sounds of her husband's boisterous laugh still echoed, but the happiness had faded in their home. She entered the master bedroom and eyed *their* bed, *his* dresser, *his* clothes that still hung in the closet. How long would she hold on in the hope that he would return, knowing he never would. In the shower, she found his shampoo still in the corner where he'd left it. Getting dressed, she found his favorite slippers in the corner of the closet under the suit he had hated to wear. In the hallway, on her way back downstairs, were family photos, their bond eternally captured, never ageing. But in real life, she'd changed her hair and Ryan had grown, yet the home had remained in the past.

Ryan's giggles traveled up the stairs and her heart ached. He deserved that, more happiness in his life. Was that her doing? Had she been holding onto the past, not allowing them to grow in life?

By the time she made it to the bottom of the stairs, she was no longer sure of what the future held, but she knew it was time to open the door.

"I'm ready," she called, but Maverick was already bulleting through the hallway, Ryan's arms around his neck.

He stopped by the front door and set Ryan down on his feet. "All right, little man. Let's get to the site. After that, I need a shower."

"You could—" As she turned to gesture to the fifteen steps he'd have to climb to reach the only bathrooms with showers, she froze.

He clasped her hands. "No worries. I could climb that without any trouble, but all my stuff's at home." He turned and winked at Ryan. "No sense in showering if I can't change my unmentionables."

Ryan roared with laughter. "Unmentionables? What's that? Underwear?"

There was something different about her son, a childishness she hadn't seen in a long time. As if the world had fallen from his shoulders and he could be a little boy again. He needed this. Even if she wasn't ready, her son needed some joy in his life.

She squeezed Maverick's hand. A gesture she hoped would speak of more than just that it was time to go. It was time to move on with her life.

He winked and brushed his lips across her knuckles. Adrenaline glittered across her arms and legs. Maybe she was ready. The man had brought a new job that allowed her to spend more time with her son, laughter to her home, hope for their future. There was no reason they couldn't try being friends, co-workers, and perhaps more. No reason at all.

CHAPTER THIRTEEN

Maverick spotted James standing outside the main hanger, looking up at the building. He hoped the old man had received his text that he'd be late. He wasn't sure why he'd stood him up to stay at Julia's but considering James's pushing and prodding to get the two of them together, he figured he'd be forgiven.

Julia helped Ryan out of the back seat while Maverick wheeled over to James. "Hey, man. Sorry we're late."

James eyed Julia and Ryan then smiled. "No worries. Deliveries were made this morning from the local lumberyard and your men in Miami. They got up here quick."

"They're good guys. They drove all night."

Ryan ran over, but Maverick held up one hand. "Hang on there, buddy. You stay with your mom. I don't know what's around the outer buildings."

Ryan kicked a rock. "Yes, sir."

The clear skies allowed the morning summer sun to beat heavy onto the asphalt. Julia pulled out some sunscreen and applied it to Ryan's face. She'd changed out of the eye-catching sundress, but the shorts showed off more of her firm legs, the t-shirt accentuating all the right places.

"You here to work, or gaze at something pretty all day?" James teased.

Maverick moved closer to the building, to where James waited at the side door, before the old man could say something else and Julia caught his meaning. "Did you get a chance to look over my additional changes?"

James nodded. "Yep, and I have something to show you. That is, if you can take your eyes off Julia for a moment."

Maverick shoved through the doorway, not willing to have that conversation, and found piles of bags, boxes, and drywall. "What's all this? I was expecting about half this."

"It turns out there are more families afflicted by the war than we initially realized. According to my contact at the VA in Riverbend, they've had calls from three counties over asking about this project. The University of Tennessee even reached out about possible internship opportunities."

"Really? But we haven't even started renovations, or have an opening date yet. Sounds like we need an organizer before the building's even finished. Do you think the county will approve the budget if we move up Julia's start date? We can document the necessity of the position with a simple letter from the VA."

James circled the stacks of materials. "I think I could get the VA to write something up. It'll come with a price, though. They still want me to work over there for a while. Apparently, the new head of the PTSD clinic didn't work out. I've told them I'll work twenty hours a week, no more since I still have my hands full with the farm, but that puts more on you and Julia. Do you think you can manage?"

Maverick couldn't help but glance out the dirty old window at the strawberry blond beauty outside. "I'm sure we can manage."

James slapped his leg and let out a hoot of laughter. "I bet you can. Looks like someone got bit by a motivation bug. You're suddenly all in on this project now. What happened?"

Maverick counted the drywall sheets and made calculations in his head. There would be enough to finish the hangar, but not enough for the outer buildings. "I said I'd do it," he replied with a shrug. "But about that leg thing. Since you said I had to utilize them if I took on this project, then I guess I need an appointment with the PT."

James rubbed his chin. "Really? The man who swore he'd never use *those blasted things* is now going to volunteer to go to therapy?"

"You said it was a requirement," Maverick huffed, "so I don't have a choice."

The back door rattled from a summer breeze sweeping down the mountains into the valley.

James rounded the supplies and peered out the window at Julia and Ryan. "Listen, I'm glad you've decided to give walking a try. You know, even if your command led to the death of your men, you received that command from higher-ups. It wasn't your fault.

It's time for you to let go of that guilt and allow yourself to live again, because that woman out there, the one you can't take your eyes off of, and that little boy who worships you, deserves a whole man. And I'm not talking about your missing legs."

Maverick wanted to be mad, he even grunted his displeasure of the conversation, but he knew James was right. "That's easier said than done when I don't believe I deserve to be alive. Not when my men are all dead." He sighed. "It took a while, but I believe there was a reason I lived. I'm doing penance by helping other men who have made it out alive, or the families whose loved ones didn't make it home. It gives me a purpose. It's the only reason that makes sense to me."

"I know." James squeezed his shoulder. "It's called survivor's guilt for a reason. But today, you're willing to take the first step toward a better life. Just make sure you're ready to include Julia in it before you get too close. She's been through enough. And her trust in men, especially men like you, is delicate."

"Men like me? What do you mean by that?" Maverick asked.

"I think I should let you ask Julia that. You two need to figure this thing out together if you want it to work. And by the look of you, you definitely want it."

Ryan busted through the front door. "Wow! That's a lot of stuff. Is that all for this place?"

Maverick shook off the whispers of regret and plastered on a smile before turning to face the little boy. "Yup. Be careful you don't trip on anything." Turning to James, he said, "Let's go over to the outer buildings and check those. It looks like we're ready for renovations. Do you think we can get some volunteers out here tomorrow after church to help clear the debris and such, get the place ready for construction?"

"I'm sure we can. With all the excitement about this project, I think we'll have people beating down our door to help. I'll call Judy while you go check the rest of the buildings. The Red Hat Society and the church can start posting and calling people. Heck, now days they all use that face thing, so they should be able to spread the word pretty quick."

Maverick bounced over the threshold back into the squelching heat. "You mean Facebook?"

"Yeah. I hear there are like ten others websites like it now. I don't know how all the young folk keep up with it all. Heck, I don't know how Judy does it, though she gets Lisa to teach her. That daughter-in-law of ours is one smart cookie."

Maverick watched Ryan hop on and off boards as Julia held his hand. "Yes, she is. And I bet she can help us with some of the furniture pieces for the homes and office."

"Oh, she's already on that. Found ten beds for next to nothing. She and Eric are working on refinishing them. Should be able to bring them here in a couple of weeks. We get our grandbaby tomorrow night while they drive to Nashville to pick up the beds. They'll spend the night and come back the next day, so we get an entire night with Amelia." James's eyes sparkled with excitement. "Although, Eric is digging his heels in. That man can't stand to leave his daughter for five minutes."

"I could see that," Julia said, stroking Ryan's hair from his forehead.

"Mama." He swatted her hand away. "Not in front of the guys."

Maverick covered his mouth to keep from laughing. James snagged his cell phone from his pocket and walked off, but not before his laughter broke free.

Ryan crossed his arms and tapped his foot. "What?"

"I'll tell you what. Sounds like you have a job to do tomorrow, if that's okay with your mom. We need to clear this property so work can start on Monday. You think you're up for it?"

"Yeah!" Ryan fisted his hand and pulled his elbow to his waist. "Will I get a tool belt?"

Maverick led them to the first barrack. "Maybe. I'll have to see what I can come up with."

"I don't know if I can be here until afternoon," Julia said. "I'll need to work on whatever Cathy has waiting for me. I'll let you know after we meet her at Café Bliss on the way home. She said she'd be there for a while when I texted her."

Maverick shoved open the door to the barrack and to his relief more supplies already sat inside. James must've directed them to the correct buildings when they arrived. Now, he felt a little guilty about being late this morning, but James didn't seem to mind. Maverick was glad James didn't bring up the fact he supposed to be there at seven for deliveries in front of Julia. "Sure, we can stop."

Julia sent the text then slid her phone into her purse.

"After that, can we go for a picnic?" Ryan asked.

"It's awful hot for a picnic," Julia said.

"Not if we go to the lake." Ryan bounced on his feet. "Come on, Mama. We haven't been in so long."

Julia toed a crack in the asphalt with her sandals, her pale pink toenails a cheery contrast to the dark broken surface. "I'm not sure."

The hesitation in her voice made his mind reel with possible reasons. Perhaps he needed to give her a way out. Maybe she wanted it to be just the two of them and he was intruding. "You two can go. I know this is your special day together. I'll take you home—"

Julia took his hand, and the light of his soul flared, out-shining the sun. "It's not that. Ryan, you sure you want to go there?"

Ryan shuffled between his feet. "We don't have to. We can go see a movie or something."

She watched her son for a moment then looked down the runway as if to search for something. "It's okay. I think it's a great idea. We'll get a picnic lunch made at Café Bliss to take with us. Sound good?"

"Sounds double-stuffed awesome!" Ryan ran to the next building and opened the door, peeked inside for a split second then ran to the next, until he reached the last structure. "They all look the same," he hollered.

"Yes," Maverick nodded.

"What'll they be used for again?"

Maverick squeezed Julia's hand. "Housing."

"Doesn't look like people could live there." Ryan's

nose crinkled.

"That's what's so great about construction and refurbishing things. You can take things that look like junk and make them amazing." The old Maverick, the one who used to get excited about new projects, surfaced, giving him a construction high he hadn't had for as long as he could remember. That was the reason he sold his company. There was no satisfaction in constructing new office buildings for tons of money. He had enough money, but not enough satisfaction. This promised to bring satisfaction and no money, and he couldn't wait to get started.

"You can do that? Coooool." Ryan hopped over a pile of wood.

Maverick reluctantly released Julia's hand to wheel himself back to the car. "Let's go. I'm excited to get some volunteers organized. Then we can get to work tomorrow."

They all piled in and waved bye to James who was still pacing around the front chatting on his phone. The AC managed to kick into full gear after a few minutes, cooling the cab by the time they reached the main road. It was a short drive to the coffee shop, but Ryan kept them entertained with questions.

"Where will they sleep? How will they get food? Who will live there?"

Maverick chuckled at his enthusiasm. He was used to gruff men and desert living, not little boys and soft touches from a beautiful woman.

When they got to town, all the parking spaces along Main were filled, so they parked on Ivey Lane and hiked over. Ryan watched each time he popped a wheelie to manage a curb. The way the boy stared, he would've thought he was piloting a space ship instead of a wheelchair.

After wading through a crowd of summer tourists, they managed to reach the coffee shop. Cathy stood and opened her arms to Julia and Ryan. A quick hug for each then they both sat down. He paused at the probing eyes of Mr. Watermore seated a few tables from theirs. Noticing Maverick, the man turned the other way. Maverick wasn't sure Julia saw him, or if she chose not to acknowledge him. Either way, Maverick didn't like his close proximity. He was usually a good judge of character and that man had villain written all over him. The way he slinked near Julia, acting like he didn't even notice, made Maverick's skin crawl. And there was no way he'd let that man get his paws on Julia again. If all went well, she would be at her new job by next week and far away from Mr. Watermore and his roaming hands.

CHAPTER FOURTEEN

"I'm sorry we're late. We were at the hanger, looking over the property for the veteran facility." Julia scooted the bag of work from Cathy to her side.

Cathy waved her hands. "No worries, hon."

Maverick hovered near the table, his wheels rocking back and forth with the movement of his hands. Julia set her purse in her lap and smiled at Cathy. Did he not want the town to know they were becoming friends?

He spun around toward the front counter. "What can I get you guys to drink?"

"It's too hot for coffee. I'll take an iced tea. Ryan'll have a—"

"Chocolate shake?" Ryan hopped twice in his seat with way too much energy.

"Nice try. You had a cupcake this morning. No one in here wants you to have even more sugar. I'll let you have a root beer, though. Not that it's much better."

"Really?" Ryan hugged Julia. "Can I come with you, Mav?"

"Mav? It's Mr. Maverick," Julia reminded him.

"If you're okay with it, he can call me *Mav*. I kind of like it." His boyish smile melted her resolve and Julia nodded. Ryan fist-bumped him before racing toward the counter. The bond between them was undeniable. He'd attached himself to Maverick faster than he had to Rusty. Could he handle another rejection? What if Maverick became involved with a woman and ended up too busy for him like Rusty did. She didn't blame Rusty for moving on with his life, or Becca for wanting to be with her soul mate, but could Julia put Ryan through that again?

"Whatcha thinkin' about, darlin'?" Cathy asked.

"Huh? Oh, nothing."

Cathy hit her palm to the table. "Don't pee on my leg and tell me it's raining."

Julia burst out a stuttered laugh. "What?"

"Stop lying, girl." Cathy leaned in, her prying poker face intact, and waited.

"I guess I'm trying to figure out if I should let that man get so close to my son. James says he's a good man, and his word is good enough for me. But what if he moves on and leaves Ryan feeling alone again?" Julia toyed with the hem of her shirt, not wanting to face the judgmental gaze of the woman.

Cathy patted her arm. "I know you love your son and want the best for him. No one's doubtin' that, Hon. But are you sure it's Ryan you're trying to protect? I saw the way you looked at Maverick. Of course, who wouldn't? He's finer than a frog's hair split three times."

"Cathy. Seriously?"

"Oh, come on, girly. You know you've got the hots for that man. You should go for it. You're single and beautiful, and I saw the way he looked at you, too." She winked. "Trust me, go for it."

Julia picked at the corner of the nail polish on her thumb, a nervous habit she'd never been able to break. Once there was an imperfection, she had to remove it from all her fingers. Another OCD issue. "Why would a bachelor that looks like him want an insta-son? Most men don't want to deal with someone else's kids."

"Look at those two." Cathy pointed at the two boys near the counter. Maverick blew through a straw, sending the wrapper into Ryan's hair. Ryan picked up his own straw and retaliated. The owner, Mrs. Fletcher, laughed and handed Ryan more ammo.

"Hey, I'm getting ganged up on. I see how it's gonna be around here." Maverick swiveled around a table and bent in half to dodge the straw wrapper shooting his way.

"I guess he does like kids," Julia chuckled. "At least, he seems to enjoy hanging out with Ryan."

Cathy waved her hand in a dismissive gesture. "Of course just 'cuz he's good looking and likes kids doesn't mean he's a good man. He could be meaner than a wet panther."

Julia kept her eyes on the straw battle taking place before her, a smile tugging at her lips. "Oh, he's not. I mean, he's a gentleman and gives back for sure. Look at what he's doing for a community he just moved to. This entire project for the veterans. I mean, I know he has a connection with the cause and all, but still, he didn't have to donate his time and expertise to this town. Oh, that reminds me, we need volunteers tomorrow."

Cathy nodded. "Already on it. Judy called me. We've already got the phone tree going. Judy's handling the Facebook posting and Karen's got the emails flying. Mrs. Fletcher offered to send sandwiches, Mr. Murdock is sending bottles of water from his store, and Rusty's delivering fruits and vegetables. That way the volunteers will have lunch before they get to work. The church van is even transporting those that can't drive over for various reasons."

"Wow. You really are on it." Julia laughed. "I hope this all works out. It's still hard to believe there's really a job that'll let me spend more time with Ryan. I just wish I knew if I'd be able to get into nursing school. I'm thinking I might need to put it off."

"Oh, honey, I thought you'd always wanted to be a nurse."

Julia sighed. "I do. It's just that, I think Ryan needs me right now. He's been a little clingy lately."

"In what way?" Cathy asked.

"Well, last week he came in my room four times in the middle of the night to make sure I was home."

Cathy tilted her head. "That is strange. Did he say why?"

Julia spotted Ryan returning and lowered her voice. "No. I asked, but he just said he wanted to check."

Maverick wheeled over and placed the glass of iced tea on the table. Ryan scooted a chair between them. "I can't believe I got cupcakes and root beer in the same day."

"Don't fill up on that, or you won't be able to eat the yummy picnic Mrs. Fletcher is making for us."

Ryan smiled then his mouth fell open and scrunched his eyebrows. "What's *he* doing here?"

Julia turned to find Mr. Watermore sitting only a few feet away. Had he been there the whole time and she hadn't even noticed? She wasn't used to seeing him in a cap and shorts. The man was always dressed in suits at work, as if his job was more prestigious than printing things for a living.

"I guess you still haven't learned any manners, young man." Mr. Watermore sneered then scooted his chair out with a loud squeal that turned the heads of several other patrons.

Julia pushed out her own chair and stood eye-to-eye with him. "You might be my boss, and I'm happy to do my job and work hard, but that doesn't give you the right to insult my son."

Maverick wheeled around the tables, but remained a few feet away, as if to give her room to deal with the issue on her own, yet close enough to jump in if needed. She appreciated that. As much as it was nice to be rescued once in a while, it was important that Ryan see her stand up to her boss, to know that she could and would take care of herself. He may be the man of the house, but she didn't need to add to her son's burden by continuing to make him worry about her.

"I was just stating a fact. Now, if you'll excuse me, I have a meeting. Not all of us have time for picnics with ill-mannered children."

Cathy's chair squealed then nearly toppled over. "I think it's time for you to leave."

"It's a public place. I have the right to be here." He brushed imaginary dust from his shirt. "You could stand to learn some manners, too. I don't know what that husband of yours was thinking, marrying a crazy old bat like you," he muttered.

"He knew exactly what he was doing. He knows better than to cross a crazy old bat who's likely to get confused between her gas pedal and brake while driving."

"Is that a threat?" Mr. Watermore sneered.

"I didn't hear a threat. Did you?" Maverick asked in a sarcastic tone.

"Nope. Just a couple town folk having a pleasant conversation," Julia added.

"So that's how it's going to be. Well, Julia if you still want your job on Monday, I expect you there at seven sharp. There's some extra cleaning we need to handle." Mr. Watermore marched past Ryan with a glower. Julia stepped between them and tucked her son into her side. It wouldn't be soon enough when she could tell him what to do with his job.

Oh, God. The job. Had he overheard their conversation? Would he fire her first thing Monday morning? If so, that job had to come through sooner than planned. There was no way she'd go back into debt.

Maverick cut Mr. Watermore's exit off. "Let me get that door for you." He opened the door, his bicep bulging against this t-shirt, his jaw clenched tight. Even in his wheelchair, Julia had no doubt he could demolish Mr. Watermore in a fight.

Julia lowered into her seat and sat Ryan on her lap.

"I'm sorry, Mama. I know I shouldn't have said that, but he gets me all fired up."

She brushed Ryan's hair from his face. "We spoke about this."

He bowed his head. "I know. I'm sorry."

"I tell you what. If you promise not to say things like that again then I promise to let this go. I know you wouldn't disobey me again."

"No, Mama. I won't." He threw his arms around her neck and in that moment, all was right.

Maverick appeared with a picnic basket on his lap and a smile on his face. "Let's not let that jer—uh, man ruin our day. He might have work, but we have some serious fun to get to."

Julia turned to Cathy as she lifted the bag of mending from the floor. "Cathy, I'll have these back to you tomorrow night."

"Oh, no need to hurry, darlin'. I'll be out of town to see my kids anyway. Devon rented a cabin in the mountains and invited my kids and grandkids. We're going to spend two whole days together. I won't be back until Wednesday night, so take your time. I already told people not to expect anything until Friday." Cathy lit up brighter than on her wedding day. But no wonder. She'd been estranged from her kids for years, but Devon must've reached out to them.

"Oh, Cathy! That's fantastic." Julia hugged her

tight. "You did marry a good man. I'm so happy for you. If anyone deserves this, you do. You sure you don't want me to get these done and deliver them for you?"

"Nope. I'll get them from you Thursday. Besides, I'll be leaving bright and early Monday morning, right after my Pilates class."

Julia still couldn't believe how much weight Cathy had lost since last year. She looked amazing. "Great. Then I'll have them ready by Thursday morning. Thanks again for letting me help you out with this. The extra money comes in handy."

"My pleasure. You do great work." Cathy slid her purse strap over her shoulder and sauntered over to Maverick. "You enjoy," she said with her southern twang on overdrive.

With a wave to Mrs. Fletcher, they all filed out the front door into the hot afternoon sun.

"Okay, let's grab your swim suits and then run by my place to get mine. I can shower later."

"You can swim?" Ryan asked.

Julia shushed him, but Maverick laughed. "Can you?"

Ryan nodded. "Uh-huh."

"Then I think we need a race. Your mom can be the judge. Who swims faster, the little man with the big attitude or the big man with the little legs?" Maverick lifted his thighs.

"You're on." Ryan cupped his hand over his mouth and whispered to Julia, "Don't tell him I was the Sweetwater County swim champ last year."

"I won't. Promise."

They reached home and Julia ran inside with Ryan while Maverick stayed in the truck to make some calls about expediting a shipment of supplies. Julia stood in front of her bed, eyeing her swim shorts and athletic top next to her bikini laid out on the comforter. Most women wore a two-piece at the lake, but was she too old for that now?

"You ready yet?" Ryan yelled down the hall.

"I'll be right there." Unable to make a decision she put on her bikini under her swim shorts and top, grabbed her bag with towels and sunscreen, water shoes and all sorts of other lake supplies then joined them in the truck.

"Okay, man. Sounds good. Yep, it'll be pro-bono work, so make sure they know that. I think we can get the inside knocked out in a week." Maverick held up one finger and mouthed *sorry*. "Okay. Yep. See you on Tuesday. Bye."

"Everything okay?" Julia asked.

"Yup. Just some old friends back home. I sold my construction company to them, so I've asked them to sponsor some guys to come up here and work for a week to get this build finished. James says he's got some other volunteers with construction experience that'll show up on Monday. We might have this place ready in a few weeks, sooner maybe."

"Really? That'd be amazing."

"I've got even more good news, but you'll have to wait until we're at the lake. It's a surprise."

"Seriously? You're not going to tell me?"

Maverick slid the gearshift into reverse and backed

out of the driveway. "Nope, not right now."

Julia turned to Ryan in the seat behind her. "Do you know what the secret is?"

Ryan shook his head. "Nope, but I hope it involves ice cream."

"Man, you have a bigger sweet tooth than I do." Maverick drove down Main then headed out of town to the lake.

The heat radiating off the highway looked like waves in the air in the distance. Ripples of some sort, like seeing the world through a funhouse mirror. For once, she wouldn't mind an afternoon storm to cool things off a bit, but that would ruin their time at the lake, so she decided she could bear the heat a little longer.

They pulled into the crowded gravel lot and made their way around several rows until a parking place became available. Men, women, and children all flocked to the lake for some summer recreation.

"I can't wait to beat you to the buoy and back. You'll never catch me." Ryan snagged his goggles out of the bag and yanked her arm toward the walkway to the dock.

Several men were standing at the top, directing people around to the long flight of stone steps on the other side of the parking lot. "Sorry. No one can go through this way," one of the men said as they walked up. "They're working down there."

"But it's the only way down to the lake." Julia tilted her head toward Maverick. If this ramp was closed, certainly they had wheelchair access somewhere.

"Sorry, ma'am. I can't let you use the ramp. They're repairing sections to get it ready for the Fourth of July celebration. Something about a structural issue." He gave her an apologetic smile. "The only way down is the stairs over there."

Julia eyed the man. He seemed familiar, the way one eye twitched as he spoke. "Hey, I know you. Don't you make deliveries to Creekside Printing?"

"Ah, yeah. That's my day job. Crowd control is more a weekend thing for me."

Maverick sat with the picnic basket in his lap, looking at Ryan with a brave face. "It's okay. Who really wanted to swim anyway."

"We can go see a movie instead," Julia offered.

Ryan raised his chin high. She was proud of him for not wanting to make Maverick feel bad, even though he'd been begging to go to the lake for so long.

Maverick handed Ryan the picnic basket. "Actually, this is a good thing. I've got something I need to take care of. Lots to do if we're going to get those buildings ready. Call me when you're ready to head home and I'll come back to pick you guys up." He spun his chair around. Rocks popped from beneath his tire and he sped away with nothing more than a backhand wave.

CHAPTER FIFTEEN

Morning light shone through the windows. Maverick sat up and eyed his nemesis, the two prosthetic legs resting in the corner of his bedroom. He'd been a coward yesterday, unable to face Julia and Ryan at the lake. If only he'd been walking, he wouldn't have had to leave them behind and beg James to go pick them up with some lame excuse about having to drive to another town to pick up some supplies. James called him out on it, but picked them up anyway.

He scooted to the end of the bed. The half-sanded walls in the one story, five bedroom house remained a reminder it was a construction zone. He'd bought it for a steal since it was at the edge of town and abandoned. It had once housed a large family, but now it needed some renovating. But despite that, the property was beautiful.

With a forced breath, he grabbed one of the legs. It was now or never. Time for him to give it a shot. He couldn't bear the thought of seeing Ryan look at him with disappointment, and Julia with her pity. It wasn't their fault. It was uncomfortable and they did their best, but he wanted to give them more.

He slid the protective sock over his stump, then the other. The room filled with bone-chilling silence, but he could imagine his men cheering him on. That was what his comrades did daily in the field, cheering each other on, supporting each other.

He slid one metal leg over the sock then the other. It fit snug, almost too snug on his right stump. After several deep breaths, he shoved from the bed and stood for a second, wobbled, then fell face first onto the floor. He punched the hard wood. "Come on! You've got this."

He held onto the bedpost and swung one leg around to the front. Keeping the left one behind him, he shoved to standing, this time keeping hold of the bed.

With his abs tight, he swayed a few times until he could manage to balance. Sweat instantly pooled at the nape of his neck, every muscle in his body tense, struggling, fighting. Flashes of waking in the hospital to the empty space under the thin sheet, his commanding officer hunched over the bed, recounting what happened. Bad Intel. Bad orders. Bad decisions.

He channeled the energy of his men, the ones that didn't make it home. He couldn't give the men back their lives, but they could still help change the future of others. He used their strength and determination, willing his right thigh to move. Tears streamed down his face, dripping from his chin. His pulse bombarded his neck with its *rat-ta-tat* firing. He swallowed the anger, the fear, the guilt, and dragged his right leg an inch then another. "For the Black Diamonds," he choked out.

He let go of the bedpost and moved his right leg a step in front of him. His arms flailed, but he didn't grab onto the bed post, or the guilt. Instead, he dragged his left leg to join his right. For a moment, he stood tall, proud. His abs vibrated with exhaustion, his thighs protested the weight pressing against the prostheses. Too tight, too wobbly, too unbalanced, he fell forward. His hands braced his fall and the left prosthetic severed from his stump.

His arms, legs, stomach, shoulders, feet, everything felt fatigued. *Feet?* He lay on the floor for a moment, exhaustion shackling him to the ground. One, two, three long breaths pressed through the resistance in his lungs. The cool air flooded inside, feeding his muscles with needed oxygen.

His phone vibrated on the nightstand. With the small amount of restored energy, he army-crawled to his bed and grabbed the phone. "Hello?"

"Hey, you headed this way soon? I want to chat with you before everyone arrives."

"Yeah. I just need to throw on some clothes. Equipment's already packed in the truck. And I want to talk to you about something, too."

"Then get yourself over here," James said, his voice light and happy.

He had to face Julia and Ryan today. It was wrong of him to ditch them yesterday, but he didn't want to ruin Ryan's special time. If only he would've been able to manage the long rocky hill or cement steps...but it wasn't practical. And it was supposed to be a mother-son day anyway.

Yes, that was what he'd say. He'd tell them he realized he was imposing on their day together, so he wanted to give them some time. That sounded reasonable. She wouldn't argue with that. He'd rather be in the captive pit, awaiting interrogation, than have Julia angry with him. He'd never groveled to a woman before. Of course, he'd never walked since his injury either. It was time for him to man-up and make some changes, changes for a real future. For Julia and Ryan. They deserved it.

He returned his prosthetic legs to their corner, tossed on his clothes and made his way to the site. The excitement of seeing Julia and Ryan bolted through him like five shots of Mrs. Fletcher's specialty espresso. It was hard to believe they'd just met. That they'd become so close so quickly. He'd never been this excited about seeing a woman before, not that he could remember.

James stood outside with two cups of coffee in his hands. Maverick hadn't even thought about coffee, or breakfast for that matter. He parked and joined James at the side of the building.

James handed him the cup and leaned against the metal siding of the hanger. "I thought you could use a cup for our conversation."

Maverick had thought he would be asking questions about the project, but based on his set jaw and pressed lips it was going to be more than that. "Okay, but I really want to ask you something first. Can you get me in to that PT friend of yours tomorrow morning? I need my prosthetics adjusted."

James choked on his coffee. When he continued to cough, Maverick smacked him in the back. "You don't have to be so dramatic. It's not like it should be a surprise. You ordered me to walk if I was going to work on this project, and I told you I would."

James wiped his mouth with the back of his hand. "You and I both know you had no intention on listening to me. I'm sure I have Julia to thank for your recent interest in coming out of your hermit state. But the way you ditched her and Ryan yesterday...that was unacceptable."

"I didn't ditch them. I thought they wanted some mother-son time, so I used the excuse of no accessibility at the lake so I could let them out of having me tag along."

James lowered his cup to his side and placed one foot behind him on the wall. "How long did you practice that line?"

"What are you talking about?" Maverick sipped his own coffee, enjoying the light roast flavor.

"Come on. You've got to do better than that. I had to guilt Julia into coming back out here today. She twisted her ankle again on the hill and she said she didn't know if she could stand that long to be of any help on the project. I had to pick them up an hour after you dropped them off. They both looked like they had a horrible time, too. Ryan just wanted to go home." James shook his head. "Good job. You proud of yourself for bailing on them now?"

"Is she okay?" Maverick sat forward in his chair, ready to jump out and run on his stumps to make sure she wasn't hurt.

"She's okay. I wrapped her foot. It's not broken, just aggravated." James gave him a stern look. "As I am with you."

"What was I supposed to do? I couldn't get down to the water."

James dropped his foot back to the ground and stepped forward. "So, you did bail because of that."

"Stop head-shrinking me. Ryan wanted to swim. I did the right thing."

"Did you? Disappointing a boy that took you to a special place, a place his father used to take him, only to have you run off?"

"It was? I didn't know."

"Of course you didn't. You were too busy trying to protect yourself from another disappointment. You're so scared about letting people down that you hide from life. I've been gentle with you so far, but you better get over yourself or you'll lose that amazing woman before you can even get something started."

The roar of a truck drew James to the corner of the building. "Looks like the cavalry has arrived. When Julia gets here, you need to tell her what's going on with you. She needs to talk, too. According to Cathy, you two are going to muck this up."

James disappeared, leaving Maverick to his thoughts. He couldn't argue with anything the man said, but that didn't make it any easier. The thought of facing Julia and Ryan, seeing their disappointment, was worse than being stripped and beaten by the enemy.

He headed for the truck, grabbed his job lists then made his way to the crowd. A few scribbles later and he had Julia, Ryan, and himself scheduled to work on the outermost building. He'd planned on being in the hanger for the big job, but today was just cleanup, so they could manage that without him.

Cathy and Devon shuffled over, carrying a long folding table. "Where do you want the food set up? Church people will be arriving soon. Pastor John ended service early after his sermon on giving. I think we'll have a few extra people showing up after that inspiring guilt trip."

Devon unfolded the table and shook Maverick's hand. "Good to meet you. I've heard a lot about you. Sorry I haven't been around more. I had some things to take care of before we left for the mountains."

"No worries. We're glad to have you here now," Maverick said.

James escorted Judy to the table and they all began setting the food out. Other people arrived and dropped off more food, then more and more. He'd never seen a town donate so much for one day.

Julia's green Oldsmobile came into view and his stomach did a fox hole dive.

"Why don't you go over and help Julia and Ryan with their stuff? I heard Julia's ankle's giving her some trouble," Cathy snarled at him.

He set the container with some sort of fru-fru salad down and made his way to Julia. Ryan hopped out, spotted Maverick but didn't say anything. He ran around the car and opened his mom's door. "You should drop the food and go. I don't think you should be on your foot all day." The little man looked troubled.

"I can take that for you," Maverick offered. "I'm so sorry about your ankle. Should I take a look at it?"

"No need," Julia said in a cold, distant tone. "James already did. He's a doctor, so I'm sure he'd know. He said I could come out today if I felt up to it."

Ryan took the large shopping bag and a container from Julia and set it down on the ground. Then he took his mother by the arm, as if to keep weight off her foot.

"Ryan, I told you I'm fine. You can relax. No one ever died of a sprained ankle."

"That's not funny, Mama." Ryan stomped his foot.

"Hey, little man. You okay?" Maverick reached for him, but Ryan moved away.

He jetted out his chin. "I'm good. I hope you got your work done."

"Listen. I owe you both an apology." Maverick took off his cap and twisted it in his hands. "I wanted to give you both some time together yesterday."

Ryan crossed his arms. "We could've gone to the movies instead. If you hadn't left, Mama wouldn't have gotten hurt."

"Ryan, that's not Maverick's fault," Julia scolded.

"If Mr. Maverick would've stayed we could've gone to the movies and you wouldn't have fallen." Ryan grabbed the bags and ran to James and Judy standing next to the table.

Mr. Maverick? His chest stung with regret.

"I'll go talk to him. He can't speak to adults that way."

Maverick snagged Julia's arm before she could walk away. "No, let him be. He has a right to be mad. I let him down. James told me that the lake is where he used to go with his father. If I had known..."

"It doesn't matter. You're not his father, and I shouldn't let my son get too close to strangers that might not be around tomorrow."

Might not be... "I'll be around tomorrow. And the next day and the next. I have no desire to leave you and Ryan."

Julia stared down at him. "You don't even know us. If you did, you would've never left yesterday. It's not your fault about my ankle, or about how Ryan is feeling. It's mine." She shook her head. "I don't know why I developed feelings for you so quickly."

"You have feelings for me?" Maverick raked his thumb over her hand, wishing he could take her into his arms and hold her.

"It doesn't matter. I have my son and that's enough for me." Julia tugged her hand free and shuffled to the food table.

Maverick raced after her. "James said I needed to tell you the truth."

She stopped. "Truth about what?"

"About why I left yesterday, why I don't use my legs, and why I'm struggling with even working on this project."

Julia turned to face him, crossing her arms over her chest. "I'm listening."

He folded and re-folded the lists in his hands, trying to find the words. "It's more than a five minute conversation. Can we talk after everyone eats? I don't want to say this wrong, and I'm scared that I will."

Julia glanced at Ryan standing between Judy and James, Cathy sneaking him a cookie behind their back.

"I promise I won't harm Ryan again. If you don't want me to speak to him, I won't. I'll do whatever you want."

Julia licked her lips and eyed him for a moment. "Okay. I'll talk to you after lunch, but it doesn't mean—"

"I understand."

She nodded then left to join the others while Maverick remained behind to collect himself. One look at Ryan explained why Julia was mad. He'd hurt her son and her motherhood walls were quickly rebuilding. He only hoped his words would be the wrecking ball.

The meal took over an hour. People trickled in and chatted. It wasn't until almost noon that a hundred or so sweaty volunteers began working.

Ryan silently trotted to his assigned station with trash bag, gloves and a bottle of water.

Maverick rolled next to Julia. Her expression was pensive and she held tight to her work gear. "Do you think he'll ever speak to me again?"

"Usually I'd say he's a kid and he'll be over it in five minutes, but Ryan's been struggling lately."

Maverick stopped beside the barrack and stuck his trash spear into a beer can. "I'm sorry I added to his struggles. I thought he really wanted to swim and I couldn't bear to disappoint him. I think I left to avoid seeing him look at me that way." He sighed. "I'm a coward."

"You're many things. Stubborn, hard-headed, and according to James impossible, but you're no coward."

Maverick leaned the trash stick against the brick soon-to-be veterans' home and faced Julia. "I need to get this out before I ruin everything. I left for selfish reasons. Facing that hill was like facing the reality that things had to change, but I didn't want them to. The idea of utilizing those prosthetic legs and trying to walk is difficult for me." He tried to explain why, but his words twisted in his throat. "I guess what I'm trying to say is that it's easier to runaway than to face something. I didn't mean to hurt you or Ryan. I understand if you don't want to see me anymore, but I'll confess that I'm prepared to work hard to win your trust back."

Julia sighed and sat on the top step. "It wasn't entirely your fault. You didn't really do anything wrong. After you left, that darn hill meant a huge obstacle in my life, too. I could've insisted that we all go, but I only suggested it and let you leave without a protest. I thought I was ready to move on with my life, to have a friend with the potential of more, but facing the place that we went as a family tore me up inside. I let Ryan down, too. He tried to have fun, but I used my ankle as an excuse to leave. I mean, it hurt, but I could've swam. I guess we both have some apologizing to do. The only problem is that I'm not sure you should apologize. You said yourself that you're not ready, and I don't know if I am either. Should I let you near my son if we might disappoint him again? He's been through enough already in his young life."

Maverick nudged closer then transferred from his chair to her side. "I think Ryan deserves happiness, and I think avoiding the possibility of heartache will only cripple him, the way that I've allowed my legs to cripple me."

Julia took his hand and his heart soared to the cloudless sky. "Let me think about it, okay? Maybe if we keep things slow. We edge into this and not complicate things too quickly."

"I can do that." He said the words, but one glance at her soft lips and he thought he'd have heat stroke if he didn't kiss her.

"Mama, I'm going around the back. Can you come with me?" Ryan eyed Maverick, letting him know it wasn't okay to be close to his mother any more. Something told Maverick it was about more than just the fact he'd left yesterday. This dug deeper, but now wasn't the time or place to go fishing.

"Yes, hon. I'm coming." Julia shoved from the steps. Maverick wanted to follow them, but he remained behind.

Ryan hopped over some boards, his foot catching the last one, and he slid. Julia grabbed him, but they both tumbled over.

"Mama, I'm so sorry. You okay? Are you hurt?" Ryan sounded hysterical, his voice several octaves higher.

Maverick vaulted into his chair and raced to help her up. "She's okay, Ryan. It's just a little fall."

Julia held her ankle and took long breaths, her face turning read. . "I'm fine, honey. Calm down. It's just my ankle. It gave way."

Ryan cried and threw himself into his mother's arms. "I can't lose you, too. Dad's gone. Rusty's gone. Now, Mav's gone. You can't leave me. You can't."

Julia rocked him while sitting half on a board, her leg still twisted under her. "Shhh. I'm fine. It's okay."

Maverick lowered to the ground and wrapped his arms around them both. "I'm not going anywhere, buddy. I'm here. I'll help you take care of your mother now."

They sat in the shade of the building for a long time, holding each other. All needing the reassurance, all for different reasons, but they were there for each other.

Finally, Ryan settled into a quiet sob and Julia relaxed in Maverick's arms. "Thank you," she whispered. "I think it's time I took Ryan to talk to someone."

Maverick sat back. "Come here, buddy." He lifted Ryan onto his lap. "You know why we are all working together to build this place?"

Ryan shook his head and took a stuttered breath.

"Because there are lots of people like you, your mother, and I who need help healing. I've struggled. Your mother has struggled. Even Mr. B has struggled. This place we're making here will help people like us. There'll be doctors, nurses, physical therapists, housing, families and people to talk to about how we're feeling. And you're going to help make that happen."

"I am?" Ryan wiped his nose with his sleeve.

"You are, and your mom will have a job here, and

I'll be here lots, too."

"You will?"

"Yep. I need some physical therapy. You convinced me to try out those legs. I need help with that. Do you think you could help me learn to walk again? Make me better?"

A smile revealed dimples in Ryan's cheeks. "I could really teach you to walk?"

"You sure can. I think we can all make each other better. Now, I know you're mad at me, but I think if I work hard enough I might—"

Ryan flung his arms around Maverick's neck, everything forgiven. Maverick held him tight to his chest until he felt safe enough to let go. Ryan wiped his tears away then offered his mom his hand. "Can I help you up?"

"Sure, hon. That would be great." Julia moved, but her right foot gave way again. She managed to twist and, with Ryan and the wall's help, she stood on her left foot, holding the right out in front of her. "Oh, okay. I admit it smarts a little."

Maverick settled into his chair and offered his hand. "Come here. I'll get you to James so he can take a look."

Julia hopped over and sat in Maverick's lap. He settled her so that he could reach the wheels and told her to hold onto his neck.

Ryan walked alongside, his eyes never leaving his mother.

"I told you I'd help with your mom. All's going to be okay now."

Ryan's face relaxed, his expression no longer that prisoner facing execution look. "I'll run ahead and tell Mr. B." Ryan bolted, his little legs carrying him quickly across the asphalt.

"Does it hurt bad?" Maverick asked, wishing he could take the pain away.

"Only when I try to walk," she whispered.

"Hey. She okay?" James called, meeting them at the edge of the hanger. The heat proved too much for many people, so they'd headed home, but others stayed to help finish the cleanup.

"I haven't been able to look at it yet." Maverick rolled to a stop and James bent down to take a look.

"Oh!" Julia cried as James twisted her foot left, right, up, and down. Maverick held tight to her small frame while James examined her.

"Looks like your cleanup project is more of an excuse to have a summer fling."

That voice. It sent a shot of battle adrenaline through Maverick's spine. If Julia hadn't been on his lap, he probably would've tackled the man. "What are you doing here, Watermore?"

"I thought this was a community event." The man waved a folder in front of his face like a fan. Another man stood beside Watermore in a suit, his attire anything but appropriate for a project like this.

"Mr. Burton, it's good to see you," Julia said, her voice strained with pain.

Ryan exited the building and froze. He opened his mouth, but looked at his mom and shut it again.

"Hello, Mrs. Cramer." Mr. Burton tipped his hat to

her. Maverick had overheard Judy and Cathy talking about the man, though he didn't appear to be the type to alienate his daughter so bad that she fled to college with her boyfriend to get away from him.

"Are you here to help with the cleanup?" Julia asked in obvious disbelief.

"No, I'm afraid not. Apparently, Mr. Watermore spoke to the town council and they offered to sell me this land cheap. We've been planning to expand our factory, but the county wouldn't sell the surrounding land to me. It looks like this could be a good option to build a new factory. Demands are increasing and I could certainly tear this down easy enough and build what I need."

"You can't do that. This property has been promised to the people of this county, to the VA and all veterans coming home, and their families."

"It was promised, but not signed yet," Watermore added.

Maverick moved forward, ready to smack that smug grin right off the man's face, but Julia set her good leg down, bracing the wheelchair to keep him where he was.

Judy came out of the hanger. James stood and waved her over. "Do you remember the papers we're supposed to sign on Monday about this real estate?"

Judy nodded, eyeing Watermore and Burton. "Yes. Our appointment's at ten then the place is officially set to be the center."

"It appears as if we might not be having that appointment," James said in a flat tone.

"Why?" Judy asked.

"Because Mr. Burton here plans on buying this property and the surrounding land to build a new factory, and the town council is agreeing to meet with him."

Maverick's blood swooshed through his ears. This wasn't happening. There had to be something he could do to stop it.

Ryan tugged Maverick's sleeve, his eyes swelling with tears once more. "That means we can't help people or ourselves get better?"

"There has to be something we can do," Maverick insisted, ready to go to war to save this place.

James shook his head. "If the council decides to sell to Burton Enterprises, there's little we can do. The project is dead in the water."

Maverick watched Watermore, the man's elation at the thought of taking this place away from them clear on his face. He wanted it to fail, but maybe Mr. Burton would listen to reason.

"Can't you find another area to build your factory? This hanger and those outbuildings are perfect for what we need. I'm sure we can work out some kind of deal with the county about the surrounding land," Maverick offered, hoping to open up some sort of negotiations.

"I don't have an issue with what you're doing here," Burton said. "I'm not sure why it's needed when the VA is just over in Riverbend, but that isn't the reason for my interest. I've been trying for over a year to relocate or extend my factory, but the county has changed zoning, upped the cost of land, and various other tactics to keep me from expanding. This is the closest property to town that isn't outrageously expensive. It is the ideal location and price point for the new factory. I didn't even know it was available until Mr. Watermore insisted I come out here with him. I thought he was crazy until I saw the property. But I really think it's ideal."

Cathy headed over from the second outbuilding.

"I think we better table this conversation until another time," James said. "If Cathy hears us, there could be blood. It sounds like our hands are tied, but I'd appreciate it if you left the premises, for your safety more than anything."

"I'm not scared of that old bat," Watermore huffed.

Mr. Burton pressed the button on his remote and his car door locks popped open. "You can walk then. I'm out of here. That woman isn't someone I want to have words with right now." Both men climbed into Mr. Burton's sports car, taking all hope of the future with them.

One glance at Ryan and Maverick knew he'd let him down, again.

CHAPTER SIXTEEN

J ulia walked up the front steps to the Benjamin home and knocked, her heart heavy in her chest.

Ryan slumped up the steps behind her, his head hanging low.

She'd spent all night consoling Ryan each time he woke screaming, each night terror worse than the last from another night terror. He'd had them before, but it was becoming an epidemic after seven nights in a row.

The counselor had said it was separation anxiety manifested by loss. Great diagnosis, but they hadn't got to the part about what to do about it. There had to be a way to stop Mr. Burton from buying that property.

"You gonna be okay here today while I'm at work?" she asked.

Ryan nodded. "Yes, but I don't know why you want to go there."

Julia combed through the top of Ryan's hair with her fingers. "I don't want to, but I have to pay bills."

"I'll pay your bills if you don't go," Maverick said, his voice a distinctive, deep, undeniably sexy tone. He maneuvered up the ramp.

"Sorry, that isn't an option. Like the last hundred

times you've offered, my answer's still the same. I'll pay my own bills."

"I thought you'd say that, but I had to try. Hey, little man. How's it going?"

"Not so good," Ryan huffed.

"You didn't sleep any better after I tucked you in last night?" Maverick circled him, popping wheelies.

Ryan shrugged. "I'm brave, I can handle it."

The front door opened to Judy's smiling face. "Come on in. We need to talk to y'all." A hint of hope flecked Judy's expression.

Ryan flew through the door, but Maverick waited behind with Julia. "Maybe it's good news."

"I hope so. It's been over a week. If only the council would hurry up and make up their mind, or give us some options."

Maverick took her hand and kissed her knuckles like he did each time she got too railed up. "Remember, we're in this together."

Julia squeezed his hand then hobbled into the living room to find Cathy, James, Lisa, and Eric. "It's good to have a lawyer for a son," Judy said, beaming.

"I'm a family lawyer, but I did reach out to a few friends." Eric rose from the couch and offered his hand to Maverick. "It's great to meet you in person."

"Good to meet you." Maverick shook his hand and wheeled into the corner by the satin chair. "What's going on?" He gestured for Julia to sit beside him then unwrapped her foot to examine it. His hands rubbed some of the soreness from the muscles along the top of her foot. She relaxed a little until she saw Ryan standing in the corner by himself.

Judy smoothed her skirt and sat down. "I couldn't sleep after finding out about the emergency town meeting being scheduled for today, so I made sure my son didn't either. We brainstormed all sorts of ways to fight this."

Julia tried to concentrate, but it was difficult to ignore Maverick's hands on her leg. "I spent all night on the computer, looking for land that Mr. Burton would be able to use."

"It sounds like none of us got much sleep." Judy rounded the table and sat on the arm of James's chair. "Son, I hope you have good news for us."

Eric scrubbed his chin. "I found out that when James originally approached the council about the land for the veterans center, there were no offers on the table. Some of the council members who are up for reelection, decided this would be a great project to show their love for the community, so they agreed. It seemed the best solution, but then Burton expressed interest in the property. Certain council members want money for their own agendas."

"So, they'll sell to him?" Judy asked. "Don't they have to honor our offer since they already accepted?"

"Not based on the wording of the agreement both parties signed," Eric said. "Each party had thirty days to back out of the deal. The council's thirty days is up at midnight tonight. That's why they called the emergency town meeting. I believe certain council members are worried about political fall out, but Councilman Rogers is pushing hard, and stirring up a lot of support for the preschool being funded with the money from the sale of the airfield land to Mr. Burton."

"Why is Councilman Rogers pushing so hard for this? Can't he find another place to have the preschool?"

Eric shook his head. "He has a child with special needs and now a baby they believe will have the same needs. He's been pushing for a special needs pre-school here in town for the past three years. He'd almost achieved it with federal and state funding, but with all the cut-backs he lost the opportunity. If they sell the land, they can shuffle money around to cover the cost of the preschool." Erik rubbed Lisa's back. "Having a child that could've died makes me feel for his cause, but I'd hate for this town to go to war between Veterans and special needs children."

Lisa gasped and clung to Eric. "That'd be terrible. What do we do?"

Eric rubbed his temple. "They've called an emergency session for two o'clock this afternoon. It'll be open to the public."

James clutched Judy's hands in hers. "Eric's right. We can't pen the town against each other. There's a critical need for both facilities in this town."

Judy kissed his cheek then headed for the front door.

"Where're you going?" James asked, standing.

"I've sat back long enough. It's time to do something. I'm going to talk to the one person that can save this town from an ugly battle that no one will win."

"Cathy isn't here. Didn't they extend their trip?"

Lisa said.

Judy slid her purse strap over her arm and put her hand on her hip. "Yes, but for once, Cathy won't save the day. That woman's off to see her family after being estranged for years, and we all know she'd give that up in a heartbeat to help this town, so no one tell her what's going on. Don't worry. I've got a plan, but you guys keep working other angles in case I can't pull this off." She disappeared out the door.

Maverick took Julia's hand and placed it on his shoulder. Ryan remained in the corner, fiddling with an army man he'd pulled from his backpack. Her cell phone beeped and she knew she had to leave, but one glance at Ryan, with a look of the world crushing the childhood from his body, made her hate herself. "I'm afraid I have to go," she mumbled to Maverick.

Lisa patted Eric's leg and went to the corner. Kneeling in front of Ryan, she said, "I hear Judy made some of her world-famous cookies. You want one?"

Ryan nodded.

Julia slipped her foot from Maverick and hobbled over to give Ryan a hug. "I'll be back as soon as I can. Okay?"

Ryan only nodded again and trotted off after Lisa.

Julia longed to spend the day with him, to make him feel safe and loved. She turned back to Maverick. "He's barely said anything for eight days."

Maverick rewrapped her foot and she reluctantly slipped on her flats. Mr. Watermore scolded her one too many times yesterday for nothing, so she knew he was getting impatient with her being out of uniform.

"I can't believe I have to leave in the middle of all this, but with the job at the Veterans Center being in jeopardy, I can't afford to risk my job at the print shop. And I'm afraid mending clothes isn't enough to pay the bills."

Maverick followed her out the front door. "I wish we were farther along here. That I could roll you off into the sunset, pay your bills and you could go to nursing school. I realize we're not there yet. And I know you wouldn't take me up on it anyway, but maybe someday."

For a second, she almost thought she could. She'd been happier over the last couple of weeks than she'd been in over a year. It was crazy, but she'd grown closer to Maverick in such a short time than she ever had with another man. She'd been friends with Henry since they were children. They dated all through high school then married. This whirlwind of feelings wasn't something she'd ever experienced, but she liked it. Julia bent over and kissed his cheek. "I look forward to that day."

Before he could reply, she shuffled down the steps on her tender foot.

"Be careful with that ankle today."

"I will," she called back before hopping in her car and driving to work.

The miles between the Benjamin farm and Creekside Printing didn't seem long enough. If Julia could've kept driving to Riverbend and beyond, she would've been happy, but that wasn't an option. Her only option was going inside to face the man that was stealing the future of every veteran in the county, herself, and her son.

She unlocked the front door and placed her purse behind the counter. The office remained dark, indicating there was no inventory this morning. He'd pulled this stunt everyday since he saw her siting on Maverick's lap at the site. Of course, the one day she didn't come in early, he'd show up and have a reason to fire her.

It made her skin skitter with microscopic chill bugs that threatened to morph into flesh-eating beetles at the thought of that man coming near her today.

The odor of printing materials and the lingering stench of Watermore's cheap cologne drove her to the back room to check supplies, anything to stay as far away from his office as possible. The morning ticked away slowly, with nothing more than busy work to keep her from going crazy. Of course, straightening stacks of paper so that they were perfectly lined up might drive some people insane, but it calmed Julia.

The front door opened and the office light flicked on. "Julia?" Mr. Watermore called out, his voice already sounding bossy and perturbed.

She left the sanctuary of the back storage room to face the threat of attitude, demeaning remarks, and sexual innuendos. Just another day at the office. "Yes, Mr. Watermore." The front area lit up with the harsh overhead florescent lighting. The weather outside had turned dark and gloomy since she'd arrived a couple hours ago.

"Why isn't the shop open? It's past time."

Julia shuffled to the counter, trying not to put too

much weight on her foot. "Mr. Watermore, you said you'd be in early for inventory this morning. You told me to meet you here before the shop opened."

"I never said such a thing," Mr. Watermore scoffed. "If you came in early, that's on your own time. I'm not paying you for that. Besides, I need you to stay late tonight. I need someone here for a delivery since I'm meeting with Mr. Burton about supplying him with all his printing needs."

"That's why you sold the town out?" Julia bit her lip, trying to keep the words she wanted to say contained.

"Don't take that tone with me." He rounded the counter, closing in on her personal space before she could retreat. His gaze traveled up and down her body, ending at her feet. "You're still out of uniform. I should fire you for that."

How many times a day was he going to threaten to fire her?

"Now that you don't have a job waiting for you at that pathetic little soldier place, you best work hard here. There are no other decent jobs right now. The unemployment rate is high, unless you want to go work a factory job."

"No."

"No, what?"

Julia swallowed her pride and the desire to throttle the man. "No, sir."

"That's better. Now, where are your heels?" Mr. Watermore's expression changed instantly from commanding boss to possessive husband. "You need to wear them."

"I can't. My ankle is still healing from when I injured it at the veteran's center."

"Well, you won't have to worry about going back to that place anyway." He slithered closer, putting a hand on the counter by her hip. "You can go home at lunch and get your heels. Trust me, you look so much better in them."

"Yes, sir." Julia shuffled back a few steps, but Mr. Watermore inched closer.

"You know, you should get married so you can have a man to take care of you. Then you wouldn't have to work so hard."

"Yes, well, that might be a good idea."

He shuffled so close his breath coated her neck in warm, spine-crawling air. "Really? Well, I'm glad you finally came to your senses."

"Yes. In fact, Maverick already offered to take care of me, and Ryan." She put extra emphasis on her son's name. "He's such a good man. Thank you for helping make me see that."

"Maverick? That cripple? What is it with you and military men? You like it rough or something?" He grabbed her arms and shook her.

She wiggled out of his grasp. "He's not like that." Julia didn't know why she was bothering to explain anything to this cretin. It was none of his business. "You're my boss, Mr. Watermore. And that's all you'll ever be, so I don't see how any of this even concerns you."

He shook his head, his nose crinkling like a Shar-

Pei. "He's not a real man. I thought you'd see that when he couldn't even take you to the lake."

Julia's mind reeled. "What?" *How did he even know about that? Wait.* "That man. Our delivery guy. You put him up to closing the ramp, didn't you?"

He fisted his hands and slammed them against the counter. "I did you a favor. You need a real man to take care of you." He slid his knuckles down her arm and she had to fight to keep down her morning coffee.

"You did this, all of this—taking over the land for the veterans center, roping off the lake—all because you think it will make me marry you? You're disgusting." She lifted her chin and pushed back her shoulders. "I'll never date you, and if you pursue this any longer I'll file a law suit against you for sexual harassment."

"You'd sacrifice all of this?" he huffed, holding out his arms to encompass the rest of the shop. "And me? For some cripple?"

Months of enduring verbal and sexual harassment breathed fire into her, sending heat over her body. Her hands fisted and her body stiffened. *Cripple?* That word, that insult toward someone she cared about fueled a notion deep in her brain and ignited it. She swung her fist, connecting with Mr. Watermore's jaw, and he tumbled backwards onto the floor. Blood spurted from his nose.

He squirmed around on the tile like a dying cockroach, with his legs in the air. "You're fired," he hissed.

She marched behind the counter, grabbed her purse, and tossed the keys to the shop on the desk with a loud clank. "No need. I quit."

CHAPTER SEVENTEEN

Maverick scooted past the mats then hoisted himself into his chair and wheeled out the door of the physical therapy gym. The relief of fresh, body odor free air greeted him in the main hall. Sweat poured down his back and neck. A shower was definitely in his future. He rolled up to James who waited for him by the nurse's station. "We should hurry. I need a shower before that town council meeting."

A nurse brought Ryan over, carrying two blown up latex gloves and a hand full of candy.

"Looks like someone had some fun while I was working hard." Maverick grinned at him.

"It was so cool. I got to see an x-ray machine and a scanner-thingy. I even met a brain surgeon." Ryan beamed.

They made their way to the elevators and pushed the button for the parking level. "How was physical therapy?" James asked.

"It was better than I thought it would be. I took some steps. It should go faster now that I'm learning to balance. Apparently, it's harder for guys like me because I have so much weight above my core. My stomach muscle spasms are screaming at me just from trying to remain upright. I guess for once being fit isn't paying off." He laughed at himself and his obsession with weight training. Although, he hadn't worked out in two days.

"You'll get there soon enough. I'll confess I caught a glimpse when I finished my meeting with the director. Why weren't you using your prosthetic legs?"

"I saw you, too. You were walking," Ryan added with a teeth-bearing grin. "I told you, you could do it."

"You were right, little man. As for my legs, the physical therapist wanted to know why I had them. She transferred in from the private sector and is still learning about the VA's bureaucratic red tape. I had to explain I was issued legs before I left Miami. She said that was an out of date methodology and that the VA is years behind in its methods. The modern way to learn is to walk on those things she had in the gym. You're supposed to start on shorter legs with training feet. They had several pairs in the PT gym, so we worked with that. She said I can practice standing on my own at home, but it'll take a while until I can go out with them due to my balance issues." Maverick shook his head. "It was kind of weird standing up, but being so short after over a year in a wheelchair and before that being six foot two, my brain is confused."

James held his hand in front of the elevator door, allowing Maverick and Ryan to exit into the parking garage first. "If I know you, you'll defy all the odds and be walking in a day or two."

Ryan bopped Maverick over the head with one of his glove balloons. "I bet you'll be walking by the 4th of July picnic. That way you'll be able to go down to the lake with Mama and me."

"Gee, no pressure." Maverick chucked Ryan under the chin with his knuckle. He clicked the button on his key fob, unlocking his truck. Ryan helped Maverick get his chair into the back seat then ran around to crawl in the other side behind James. "How did your meeting go?" Maverick asked as they pulled out of the parking garage. "Did the director have any suggestions?"

James pinched the bridge of his nose. "I'm afraid nothing useful. The VA doesn't want to take on Creekside. They've suggested we relocate our project."

"Did you tell them that the air field is the only location around these parts that we could modify?"

"Yes. They suggested that we ask for an alternate property from the county and build from the ground up."

Maverick turned onto the main road heading back to Creekside. "Don't they understand we don't have the funding to build? Most of our supplies still sitting in that hanger bay are donated. This is a project with a thin budget already."

"They know, but honestly, the Veterans Administration Hospital doesn't want the negative publicity that would ensue over hindering the construction of a special needs preschool." James rolled his eyes. "But hindering the completion of a Veterans center, now that won't hurt their image."

"I have to admit that doesn't sit well with me

either," Maverick said. "But there has to be an alternate solution. If we can't find one for the Veterans center, maybe we can for the preschool."

"You just need a building somewhere in Creekside that has enough room, right?" Ryan said.

James sighed. "If anyone would know of a building like that it would be Cathy. I know Judy doesn't want to bother her, but if anyone could come up with a solution, she could."

"You can't call her?" Maverick asked.

"Even if I wanted to, she's in the mountains with no cell reception. Judy has a contact number for the cabin, but she won't give it to me." James sighed again. "I love that woman, but she's as stubborn as they come. Of course, her determination is part of the reason I fell in love with her."

Since it was already late morning, very little traffic passed on the road to Creekside. "We better think fast since there is only a couple of hours until the meeting."

Ryan shifted forward as far as his seat belt would allow. "Wouldn't the parents want their kids closer? There are so many buildings already in town. Can't they use one of those for the preschool?"

"Buddy, you make perfect sense. I just wish adults thought like that," Maverick said

James rubbed his ear. "You know, there has to be a way to show them that they could utilize an existing building while saving money. And as a county, we could all pitch in to raise funds for the preschool. But that councilman won't go for it."

"Why?" Ryan huffed.

"Because he's been waiting a long time to make this happen. When he was elected, he swore he'd establish a special needs school here in Creekside, instead of having to drive kids two towns over every day. He's not going to take a chance of funds falling through again when he is guaranteed money from the land sale."

"Adults are silly." Ryan leaned back against his seat and adjusted his seatbelt.

They drove in silence for the next half hour, Maverick's mind plotting and planning several different scenarios he could present for the council. But he couldn't pull any of them off by the time the meeting started. "Sorry, guys, but I need to stop by my place for a quick shower then we can head over to the meeting."

"Sure. We should have time, but I want to get there early," James reminded him.

"Hey, Mama's car isn't outside the print shop." Ryan pressed his nose to the window, his seat belt tucked under his armpit.

Maverick swerved, trying to see for himself.

"Hey, eyes on the road," James teased.

"Maybe she went out to lunch."

Ryan sat forward again. "No, she never leaves. Her boss is mean and only gives her a few minutes to eat. She always packs her lunch. Mr. B, can I have your phone?"

"Sure, if you sit back and wear your seatbelt properly."

"Yes, sir."

Maverick didn't like the sick feeling in the pit of his

stomach, but he knew there was no real reason to worry.

"She's not answering," Ryan said, his voice quivering. "Mama, where are you? Please call Mr. B's phone."

James reached back and took the phone. "Don't worry. I'm sure she's fine. Maybe she went to run an errand."

Maverick glanced back at Ryan. The little guy had his cheek pressed to the side window. Tension and worry filled the cab of his truck. "I tell you what. We'll drive over after the meeting to check on her. We can't go inside, but I'm sure her car will be there by that point."

Still, Ryan didn't say a word. Maverick worried he'd have another fit like last week. The loss of his father obviously had taken its toll on him.

Maverick pulled into his drive and hurried inside. "I won't be long." He longed for the day when he could hop out and run up the stairs. Some of the other vets at the therapy gym were already running on the treadmill. He'd get there then he'd dance with Julia the way he'd wanted to since the moment he met her.

He passed the three bedrooms he hadn't touched since moving in, heading to one of the larger rooms in the back. It was an older home with hardwoods and not a lot of amenities, but he knew he could fix it up and sell it for a big profit. A restored home with tons of character, especially one with this many rooms and all on a single level, would resale well when the market returned. He'd already widened the doorways to accommodate his chair, so it would make a great home for an older couple or a large family.

After showering and throwing on some fresh clothes, he raced out the door, surprised to find James and Ryan weren't in the truck. The sky had darkened, warning more rain was headed for Sweetwater.

"I'm ready," he called out and locked his front door.

James came around the corner the house, rubbing the back of his neck while eyeing the sky. "Looks like a bad storm. People get nervous around here when the sky gets that color, after last year's tornado nearly demolished this town. I'm not sure if the meeting will still happen."

"If it doesn't, that'll just buy us more time," Maverick said.

James half-grinned and half-shrugged. "Or a chance for Mr. Burton to seal the deal quietly."

"There is that." Maverick glanced around. "Where's Ryan?"

James turned and pointed to the old swing set the former tenants had left behind in the side yard. "He's right..."

Maverick scanned the swing set and the surrounding lawn. Only empty swings, one still swaying.

James spun around in all directions. "He was there a minute ago. Ryan!"

No answer.

Maverick went to the other side of the house. "Ryan? Where are you, buddy?" Both men raced around the house then back to the car. "Where can he be?"

James shook his head. "He was right near me. I only took my eyes off him for a minute."

"No one could've taken him. The truck's blocking the drive and the yard's too big for someone to sneak up without you noticing. There's only one real possibility. Ryan ran off, but why?" Maverick scanned the street and house again. "Julia. He was freaked out about her car not being at the print shop. I bet he went to check on her. It's only a few blocks over. Because of the creek and fences, he'll have to stay on the main road, so we'll see him if he's walking. Let's go."

They watched out the windows, continuously scanning up and down the street while Maverick backed out of the driveway. "Should we call Julia to see if he's with her?"

James shook his head. "Not yet. There's no reason to worry her if she's not at work and we find Ryan there. We'll call if he's not."

Maverick turned down the side street and headed to Main. Two cars were parked outside the print shop, neither were Julia's. "We best go inside and ask Watermore if he's seen him."

James wrung his hands. The poor man obviously felt terrible about Ryan skipping out on him. Maverick was frightened, too, but his military training kept him focused on his mission. James had the same training, but it had been a long time since he'd served.

A customer Maverick didn't recognize turned away from the counter and headed for the door just as James entered. The man said *hello* to James, but averted his gaze from Maverick.

Seeing Maverick wheel into his shop, Watermore's eyes shot wide and he backed away from the counter. "Listen, I don't know what she told you, but it's a lie. I don't need to touch that woman. Besides, she assaulted me. Look at this." He pointed to his face.

Maverick's blood pumped through his ears, deafening him. "What did you do to her? Where is she?"

"I'll tell you the same thing I told that troublemaking brat of hers. I don't know, but she isn't here."

James stepped in front of Maverick to stop his advance. "Did he say where he was going?"

"No, and I don't care. Now, I need to get to the council meeting, so you need to leave." Watermore rubbed his jaw and Maverick noticed his swollen nose and eye. Good for Julia. He'd hug her when he saw her. If she didn't knock him out for losing her son first.

"The meeting," James groaned, massaging his scalp as if to relieve some hidden pain.

Maverick wheeled closer to Watermore, but James stayed right beside him. "If I find out you did anything to Julia, I'll come back here and teach you how to treat a lady."

Watermore stormed past and opened the front door. "This is my store, and I can refuse service. Get out. Now."

James eyed the man then turned to Maverick. "Let's go. We need to find Ryan."

He was right. Nothing was more important than finding Ryan and making sure Julia was okay. "It's time to call Julia."

They went to the truck and scanned both sides of the street before climbing into the cab. James pounded his fist against the dashboard. It was the first time Maverick had ever seen the man anything but serene.

"Don't worry, we'll find him. We'll look on the way to the meeting. I'll try calling Julia again. He's probably headed home. We would've seen him on the way here if he headed back toward my place." Maverick put the truck in reverse then dialed Julia. It rang so many times he'd turned onto Main street and headed into downtown before a recorded message said, *This mailbox is full.*

"I'm not sure what's going on, but we need to find Julia and Ryan." They passed J&L Antiques, Café Bliss and the other stores in town, but there was no sign of Ryan on the sidewalks. The quiet in the cab only added to the stress. "Listen, I'll drop you off at the meeting then head to Julia's. If they're not there, I'll go to Café Bliss and ask Mrs. Fletcher if she's seen either of them. I'll call you if I find anything. You check with everyone at the meeting and see if anyone has seen them."

James rubbed his hand where he'd hit the dashboard. "Stay in contact."

"I promise." Maverick tried to keep his brave face on while James got out, but inside he was screaming with terror. He squealed out of the parking lot, bounced over a curb, and rounded the corner to Julia's. But her driveway was empty when he arrived. He parked and walked around to make sure Ryan wasn't sitting outside, but there was no sign of him either.

Rain began to drizzle and thunder clapped in the distance. He dialed her phone once more, but it only rang. "Where the hell are you?" he whispered.

CHAPTER EIGHTEEN

Rain pelted the tin roof of the Benjamin farm's front porch, creating a soothing harmony. Julia rocked in the white porch swing and watched the rain storm blow in over the open pasture. Peaceful, quiet, nothing like her life had been the last few months.

James's car sat in the drive, but no one had answered the front door, so she sat there swaying, waiting for them to return. They were probably still at Maverick's rehab appointment in Riverbend, or on their way to the council meeting. She couldn't face the meeting, not after just losing her job and having no means to support her son. "I'm sorry, Henry. I thought I was strong enough."

Tears pooled at the corner of her eyes. "If only I held my temper." She buried her face in her hands and sobbed, the tears running down her face faster than the rain hit the grass.

A car sounded in the distance, so she wiped her tears and put on her brave face for Ryan. Now wasn't the time for her to fall apart. She needed to make him feel secure, especially with the way he'd been acting lately.

She stood and brushed off her skirt. After fixing her hair, she hobbled to the edge of the porch. Maverick's truck soared over the hill at break-neck speed and landed on the other side with an earthshaking thud. Something was wrong.

The truck slid to a stop. When she saw that only Maverick was in the car, she ran out into the rain to meet him. "What's wrong?"

Maverick opened the door and shifted in his seat to face her. "Is Ryan here?"

"What? No, he's with James. And I thought James was with you."

Maverick tugged her against him and hugged her tight. "I thought something happened to you. You're not answering your cell."

"My cell? Oh, dang. I must've left it on the counter when I stormed out of the shop."

His arms released her, but he held tight to her hands. "Listen. I don't want you to freak out."

"Oh my God. Where's Ryan?"

"He was with James at my house, but he took off to find you. We drove by the print shop on the way to my house and when Ryan noticed you weren't there, he asked to use James's phone. When you didn't answer, he became upset. I thought I'd calmed him down. I should've realized he was in distress, but I told him we'd go straight to the print shop on our way to the meeting after I showered. That way he could relax when he saw your car had returned. When I finished getting ready and came out of the house, James said he was on the swing, but he wasn't. He'd disappeared."

The rug had been pulled out from underneath Julia's life once already. She didn't think she could survive a second time. Her heart pumped adrenaline into her body like a nuclear reactor about to go into meltdown. "Could someone have taken him?" Her hands shook, but Maverick held them tighter.

"No, we know he made it to the print shop. Watermore told us he'd been there, but left."

Julia shook her head. Her breath beat against her ribs, but it couldn't escape. Her head became light and she fought to remain standing. "Home. He must've walked home from there."

"No, I went there first."

Water poured down her cheeks. She swiped at her eyes and looked around as if he'd magically appear in the front pasture. "Town? He's at the café or one of the shops."

Maverick tightened his grip. "I checked. Julia, think. If Ryan is really upset and he can't find you, where would he go?"

Ideas flew through her mind, but she couldn't slow them enough to grasp one.

"Calm down. We'll find him. You need to take a deep breath. Do you have a favorite spot? Where do you two go most?"

"Café Bliss." She slid one of her slick hands from his and swiped her soaked hair from her forehead.

"Okay. What about special weekend dates? Do you think he would've tried to go to the movies?"

"No." She shook her head, her bottom lip trembling. "I don't know."

"Don't worry, we'll find him. He's got to be within walking distance."

"What if he tried to hitch a ride? What if someone bad picked him up?" Julia struggled to keep her breathing steady.

"If he hitched a ride, someone in town would've picked him up and they're probably trying to call you right now. Or Ryan has tried to call you."

"We've got to go to the shop and get my phone."

Maverick waved her to the other side of the car. "We can't. Watermore is at the meeting. We'll have to go there."

Julia ran around the car and hopped in. Maverick drove them back to the highway. Unable to hold back any longer, the storm blew in with a mighty vengeance, hammering water against the windshield.

"He's got to be okay. He has to be. I can't lose him, too." She didn't know who she was even talking to, and didn't care, just as long as someone found her son.

"He's here," Maverick said. "And he's waiting for us to find him. We'll get your phone and we'll bring him home. Don't let any other thought enter your head."

She lifted her chin and reached her hand across the bench seat. His hands were busy with the hand pedals, but at the next stoplight, he took them and kissed her knuckles. "I promise we'll get Ryan back. I won't fail this time."

Fail this time? What does that mean? But she didn't have the time or energy to concentrate on anything but Ryan right now. She kept her gaze out the window, straining to see past the water running down the glass. "He's got to be soaking wet, tired, hungry, scared and confused."

They pulled into the town offices and she leapt from the car, sprinting to the front door despite her injured ankle. A secretary halted her at the front. "Can I help you?"

Julia swiped water from her face. "I need to find Mr. Watermore. Now."

The woman took a few paces back and held her hands up. Julia knew her, but couldn't think of her name. "I think you should calm down, Mrs. Cramer. You don't want to make a scene, especially with half the town in the meeting."

She eyed the double doors. "You can move out of my way or I'll take you down. Your choice. My son is missing and I need to find Mr. Watermore."

Maverick smashed through the front doors. "Did you find him?"

"Ryan is missing?" the woman asked.

"Yes, we're trying to find him," Maverick said.

"Well, I'm sure he's—"

Julia didn't have time to deal with her. She shoved past and raced to the large room, flinging the doors open. She scanned the crowd until she spotted her ex-employer. "I need my phone, you monster."

He shot up and held his hands in front of his chest. "I don't have your phone."

"It's at your shop. I left it behind after you tried to sexually assault me at work!"

The crowd gasped, but Julia didn't care. She didn't care about anything except finding Ryan.

Mr. Watermore faced the crowd of people and pointed at her. "This woman's mad. She's crazy and delusional. She went nuts in my store and punched me. Look at what she did." He shoved his face out, trying to give everyone a better look at his busted nose.

"That's right. I decked you after you groped me and called Maverick a cripple. You should be ashamed of yourself," Julia said as she advanced.

He shuffled away from her. "You see? She's crazy. I want the police to arrest her."

Julia felt the urge to ram him. "Arrest me? All I want is my cell phone so I can find my son."

"Mama?"

Julia spun around. Ryan stood behind her a few feet away. She dropped to her knees with a loud, echoing thump. "Ryan?"

"You all heard her confess to punching me," Mr. Watermore continued to snivel. "I'll have her arrested for assault. See how crazy she is?"

"Shut up and sit down," someone yelled. "You should be embarrassed that a woman decked you, not shouting it all over the town. Besides, the entire county knows you're scum. If you want my business you'll be quiet."

Maverick swooped in and tucked them both into his sides. "Thank the Lord you're both safe."

James cleared his throat. "I texted you."

"I didn't get it."

Julia held tight to Ryan, tears flowing once again. She was drenched, make-up ran off her eyes and her hair was plastered to her head, but she couldn't care less. "Where were you? I thought you were out in the rain, alone and lost."

"No. I went to find another place to have the preschool so that we could keep our project, and you wouldn't have to work for him anymore." Ryan pointed a tiny, accusatory finger at Mr. Watermore.

"Oh, honey. I told you I could handle myself, and I did."

"I know. I'm sorry, but I wanted you to have that new job, and for us to help people and to give back like Daddy did." Ryan rubbed a small fist into his eyes, wiping his own tears away.

"You're such a smart, brave boy." Julia hugged him tight to her chest.

"No, I'm not." Ryan lowered his head. "I didn't find another place. I asked Ms. Trianna if we could use the senior center, but that man back there said it wouldn't work." Ryan pointed to one of the councilmen sitting behind the long table on the platform.

Julia released him and pushed his hair from his forehead, inspecting each feature to make sure he was okay. "You tried, honey. That's all that matters. We'll figure something out."

"That means you have to go back to work at the print shop." Ryan's voice cracked. "I don't want him hurting you. I don't want to lose you, too, 'cuz then I'll be an orphan, and Mean Mike said nobody loves orphans."

Julia held his arms tight at his side. "Oh, honey. Nothing will happen to me."

Maverick leaned over and held Ryan's chin in his

hand. "Nothing will happen, but even if it did, I'd take care of you. And if I couldn't, you still have James and Judy and Lisa and Eric and Cathy and Devon and Rusty and Becca all fighting over who would get to raise you. You have a huge town family."

Ryan lifted his head. "Really?"

"Really."

"I'd rather live at your house," Ryan whispered. "I like your swing set and it's close to town."

Maverick leaned against the arm of his chair, his face tight, his eyebrows pulled together.

Julia released Ryan, but kept holding hands with him, not wanting to let him out of her sight. "What is it?" she asked. "What's wrong?"

Mr. Burton cleared his throat. "I don't mean to be rude, but can we get on with this? I need to get back to work."

"Of course, Mr. Burton," one of the councilmen said. "If you can take your family matter outside, then we can get back to business."

Maverick wheeled to the front. "If I may, I believe I have a solution, something that will make everyone— the council, the city, the children with special needs and the veterans—happy."

CHAPTER NINETEEN

Why hadn't he thought of it before? The swing set, the property, the fact it was one story and had several rooms, each of them a good size.

Maverick cleared his throat. "I believe I have a perfect place for the special needs preschool and best of all, it'll be free to the council."

"Where is this place?" a woman with short, wheat-colored hair in tight curls asked into the microphone set on the table in front of her.

Maverick pushed his shoulders back and faced the council. "That's the best part. It's just on the edge of town, but there is plenty of land for children to play. There's even a swing set."

"It sounds perfect, but I don't know of any building like that and I've lived here all my life," the councilwoman said.

"It's not a building. It's a house. The house I purchased a few months ago. It still needs some renovations, but I'll finish them and donate the property to the city for the school. It has several rooms large enough for classrooms and it'll be wheelchair accessible. It has a full kitchen for snack time, two bathrooms, a swing set, and plenty of room to add other amenities the preschool might need. If anything else needs to be added, I know I can get some volunteers and have the supplies donated to expand.

"That sounds perfect. What do you say, Councilman Rogers?" she asked.

"No."

Maverick thought he'd heard wrong, but the smile on Mr. Burton's face made him face the truth. "May I ask why?"

"Because it's not just the building that's needed. We need funding for teachers, supplies, maintenance on the facility, utilities, and other bills. The sale of the land where the old hangar is will more than fund the school for five years. That'll give us plenty of time to look into other funding."

"Yes, but if you build, that's going to take a sizable chunk out of any profit you'll get from the sale." Maverick looked toward the crowd, hoping he could win over enough of the town people to sway the council.

"With Mr. Burton's offer," Councilman Rogers countered, "we can still budget for five years."

Maverick felt the joy of finding Ryan fade from his soul. He thought he'd saved the day, the project, and the town.

"Now if you'll excuse us, we'll put the sale of the property to a vote. I'd like to remind everyone in the room that the sale of this property will provide for our special children in Creekside for several years. Our town will finally have a way to support those families that struggle day-to-day with finding trained and compassionate childcare for our children. I urge you to vote yes for the children of Creekside."

"Before you vote, there's someone here that would like to speak to Mr. Burton," Judy Benjamin's voice carried above the low mumbling in the room.

Maverick eyed the council members and Mr. Burton, both caught off guard by the intrusion.

Councilman Rogers smacked a gavel against the table. "We're done hearing—"

"Rose?" Mr. Burton left the podium and walked down the aisle. "What are you doing here?"

Rose raised her chin. "I came to see you Dad. I thought it was time we worked some things out."

Mr. Burton gave his daughter a tentative hug then stepped back, his head down. "It's good to see you. As soon as I'm done here, I'll clear my schedule and we can—"

"I can't." Rose pushed her shoulders back. "You've always set an example that we need to work hard and make things happen. In this case, that's what I'm doing. Mrs. Benjamin explained the situation to me about the land. I understand why you want it, and I don't blame you, but I'm asking you not to buy it."

"What? Why does it matter?" Mr. Burton asked, a strange softness to his voice.

Maverick edged closer so he could hear better. Julia stood with Ryan in front of her. Judy had slipped away and now stood by James's side. All eyes were on Mr. Burton and Rose.

Rose took her dad's hands in hers. "I know what I

want to do. During school, I volunteered at a clinic for children with learning disabilities. By the end of the semester, I knew I wanted to work on nutrition for children with various challenges. It's proven that diet change can affect behavior."

"That's wonderful. You can come back and work for the new pre-school once you're done with college. You'll be back in Creekside. This sale will provide the funding for that program." Mr. Burton lifted his head, a bright smile on his face.

"No, Dad. I won't sacrifice another service that's desperately needed in Creekside. I know you don't like Marcus, but I love him. We'll be getting married when we finish our first four years of school. After that, he's going into the military so he can attend medical school. He wants to be a doctor, and there's no way we can afford to send him to school for that long. Even with grants, we'd end up so far in debt that we'd spend the rest of our lives paying it off."

Mr. Burton's smile faded. He opened his mouth, but Rose held up one hand. "This isn't about Marcus and me, but about everyone that has been and could be affected by war. As a town, we shouldn't have to fight for one thing. We should join to make them both happen. If you refuse this sale, then the council will be forced to find another way. I'll personally help by coming home on holidays, and next summer I'll take the semester off to work here. As a town, we can make this happen."

Councilman Rogers stood up. "Mr. Burton, I appreciate your daughter's vision, but I've been trying to establish a preschool here in Creekside since my son was first born. He's now four. It's too late for him, but our baby is now showing signs of autism. We won't be able to wait another four years."

Mr. Burton looked down at his daughter then back at Councilman Rogers. "If my daughter says she can make it happen, I believe her."

Rose threw her arms around Mr. Burton. "Thank you, Dad."

He kissed the top of her head. "I'm not going to choose my business over you or your mother any longer. I'll find another place for my factory."

Councilman Rogers lowered to his seat, his head in his hands. The sorrow on his face tugged at Maverick's heart. They'd saved the Veterans center, but left the preschool open for failure.

"Councilman Rogers, I'd still like to donate my home. I'll do all the necessary upgrades and extensions free. The people of Creekside are a family, and as a family, I know we'll make sure our children are well cared for. I'd be happy to sign the papers now and the preschool can start as soon as you find some teachers. That means your son can attend for one year at least, until he starts kindergarten and your other child can be there also."

Councilman Rogers nodded. "I guess it's our only hope at this point."

"You're going to let that outsider, that cripple, take the school away from you?" Watermore shouted.

"Mr. Watermore, no one is taking the school away from us. This town will have both a veteran's center and a special needs preschool, which is more than we'd have if we'd listened to your nonsense," the councilwoman said. "And I'm not sure about the rest of this town, but I'll be taking all my printing needs to Riverbend." She smiled at her fellow councilmen. "I believe the council will also agree to send our city's work there as well."

"What? You can't do that. I'm the only printer in town."

The councilwoman smiled. "You're also the only man in town that will be facing charges for sexual harassment in the workplace. However, if you want to make a public apology to Mrs. Cramer and Mr. Wilson, perhaps they would be willing to drop those charges."

"What? I don't owe them an apology for nothing." Watermore stormed out of the room, his orange comb over flapping on top of his head.

Julia lowered to the ground. "I guess you have your wish, honey. I won't be returning to work. He fired me after I decked him, but don't worry. It sounds like the project is going to happen after all. Thanks to Maverick saving the day. He's the town hero."

James took Ryan by the hand. "I'm not letting go of you, little man. I can't lose you again. You two go get cleaned up and meet us at Francisco's. I'm taking us out to celebrate."

Julia kissed Ryan on the cheek. "You sure? Maybe you should stay with me."

Ryan smiled. "Don't worry, Mama. Nothing will happen to me."

"You're right." She gave him a big hug. "I double-stuff love you."

They followed James, Ryan, and Judy out to the parking lot. Only after Ryan was safely belted into the back seat did she let Maverick pull her toward his truck.

Maverick drove Julia home where she showered and gave Maverick a change of clothes. "They were Henry's, but I don't think he'd mind."

After he'd changed, he found Julia on the couch. "You ready?" he asked, wheeling over. She glanced up and put her hands on his thighs. Her expression looked as gloomy as the storm clouds overhead and he feared she'd start crying again. He wanted to sit by her side and hold her tight to him, but he stayed put, letting her collect herself.

She brushed her thumb back and forth on his leg, making it difficult for him to concentrate. Then she took a deep breath. "You know Henry died in battle and that we've had a rough time with his loss. It is not just the loss of Henry, though. It's how he died, how my grandfather died, how my father died, how my brother died."

Maverick squeezed her hands in support, knowing this was something that was hard for her to say.

"My grandfather died in World War II. He was a hero. My father died in the line of duty as a police officer. He also died a hero." Her pupils shrank a little smaller, her hands trembled. "My brother died while defending his girlfriend at a bar, a hero for protecting the woman he loved."

Every man in her life was a hero. How would he

possibly compare? A man who failed as a squad leader, friend, and man?

"Henry died overseas doing what he loved," she continued, "serving his country, protecting our freedom. He died a hero, that's what Ryan knows. What I never told him was that he didn't just die in a firefight. He volunteered to go on a mission he knew he wouldn't return from. In the end, he died by friendly fire." She took a stuttered breath. "I've lost too many men in my life to heroism. When I met you, I knew instantly you were one, too, and I tried not to care about you. I tried not to want to be around you, but apparently, Watermore was right about one thing. I have a thing for heroes." She chuckled softly.

"I'm not a hero," he muttered. "Julia, you don't know everything about me."

"Of course I don't. We're still getting to know each other. But I know you're a hero, regardless of your past. Only a hero would donate his home to the city."

"Stop saying that." Maverick pulled away and scooted back.

Her forehead crinkled and her bottom lip protruded. "I know you've been through a lot." Her eyes looked caring and sorrowful, sorrowful for his missing legs, for the idea that he did something heroic and sacrificed himself for others. But he hadn't.

"I could've been the man that killed your husband."

Julia gasped. "What are you talking about? You were there? When Henry died?"

"No." Maverick held his head in his hands. "I'm not

explaining it right. I...I sent men to their death. I relayed an order that I knew would get us all killed. Yet, I didn't do anything to stop it. I was the only one to survive. I made my choice, but my men...they didn't. They never got the opportunity to choose. Those men died because of me. I'm not a hero. I'm a murderer." He heaved, his ribs constricting.

Julia's hand grazed his face and she gently nudged his chin up. "You didn't kill those men. You were just following orders."

"I—"

"You said that your men didn't have a choice, yet you did. But did you really? What would have happened if you had ignored your orders? No, you didn't kill Henry and you didn't kill those men. It's war. Bad things happen." Julia knelt on the floor and wrapped her arms around his neck.

He pulled her tight to his chest and breathed the soft floral scent of her hair, the fresh smell of clean clothes and the aroma of forgiveness. If only he could forgive himself.

EPILOGUE

Summer lightening flashed in the distance, but it was far enough away to continue the 4th of July festivities. Julia followed Maverick down the ramp, with Ryan in his lap. The wood slats vibrated his prosthetic legs against the footplates of his wheelchair.

Sheriff Mason tipped his hat. "Hey, Maverick. I see you've got your legs on. It's a great day for it."

Trianna gave Julia a quick hug. "It's great to see you guys here this year."

Julia smiled. A piece of her heart would always remain with Henry, but the rest swelled at the sight of her friends, family, and new love. "It's good to be here."

Maverick kissed her knuckles, as he often did, and then released her to go over to their picnic spot.

Judy and James, Cathy and Devon, and Eric and Lisa with Amelia crawling between them, all waited on blankets spread out in a prime spot on the bank of the lake.

"It's about time you three got here. We were about to send out a search party," Cathy teased.

The smell of citronella and sunscreen filled the air. Tall Tiki torches lit the beach and field. As sunlight faded, a band on stage at the foot of the hill strummed to life.

Julia sat with her legs tucked under her, her pale-green summer dress spread over her legs. "I'm afraid it's my fault. I've been working on some grants. Trianna was an amazing help with that. Also, I needed to finalize the opening day schedule."

Ryan hopped down from Maverick's lap. "Hey, can I go find Thomas? He said we could play ball."

"Stay where I can see you, okay?" Julia said.

Ryan threw his hands by his side. "Oh, Mama, don't be silly. I'll be fine. I'll stay on the field or beach."

"As long as I can see you," Julia repeated.

"Ooookay." He sprinted across the field to the edge of the beach where he found his friend, Thomas, and three other boys.

"It's good to see him branching out." Maverick lifted one of his legs and flipped the foot pedal up then rested his foot on the ground. "I have to admit, it's not all about him feeling better. I selfishly want some alone time with my beautiful woman." He moved the other leg free then shoved from the chair, but wobbled.

Cathy gasped as Eric reached out to help.

"I've got this." Maverick steady himself then held out his hand with a slight bow. "May I have this dance?"

Julia looked up at Maverick for the first time. Her lips pulled back into a wide, goofy smile. "I didn't know you were so tall."

Everyone laughed.

Judy scooted into James's arms. "You haven't seen

him stand yet?"

"Nope. He wouldn't even let me go to physical therapy with him the past few weeks." Julia laced her fingers into his. "I thought he was months from being able to walk."

"I'm limited, but getting there." He took her hand and put it on his shoulder then wrapped his arms around her middle. "A little birdie told me you like to dance. If I can learn to walk, I can learn to dance. And maybe with these new legs I won't have two left feet."

James smacked his knee. "Maybe I need some artificial legs. Then Judy's toes wouldn't hurt so much when we dance."

Judy shook her head. "I think I'd take the sore toes. No injuries allowed around here for the next ten years. At least. Got it, Mister?"

"You're the boss." James kissed her cheek and took a sip out of his red solo cup.

Maverick held Julia to his chest, their hearts beating together. She thought she would lose her balance from being dizzy with happiness.

"I'm the luckiest man alive to have you in my life," Maverick whispered into her ear. "You're the strongest, most courageous, loving and supportive person I've ever met. To think, a few years ago I almost married the wrong girl. I think losing my legs showed me who we were together. Now that I'm here and I have you in my arms, losing my legs is a small price to pay to have you."

Julia held him close, despite the sweltering heat. The rest of the group's attention had moved to Amelia, everyone cooing at her as she did adorable baby things. Grateful for a bit of privacy, she asked, "How's it going living with James and Judy?"

"It's been fine. I'm looking for a new house to restore, one that I can have a family in some day."

"Oh, really?" Julia teased.

Maverick continued swaying, but he tipped her chin up. She could see the seriousness in his eyes. "According to the town motto this is the place my heart and home belong. And I'm inclined to agree."

Electricity jolted through her body. The thought of Maverick remaining near her indefinitely sent her heart into a frenzy. "I think you'll have no trouble finding something."

"Good, because as soon as I'm done renovating the house for the preschoolers, and once the Veterans Center is open, I want you and Ryan to help me find a new home where we can live together some day."

Julia stared at him with the same seriousness. He wrapped one arm around her back and tipped her chin a little higher. She stood on her toes and their lips met. Fireworks exploded overhead as the band continued playing the national anthem.

His kiss sent her body into a celebration of freedom—freedom from guilt, freedom from doubt, and freedom from fear. But most of all, the freedom to love again.

THE END

ABOUT THE AUTHOR

Ciara Knight writes to 'Defy the Dark' with her young adult speculative fiction books. Her most recent international best-seller, Pendulum, scored 4 stars from RT Book Reviews, accolades from InD'Tale Magazine and Night Owl Top Pick. Her young adult paranormal series, Battle for Souls, received 5 stars from Paranormal Romance Guild and Night Owl's Top Pick, among other praises.

When not writing, she enjoys reading all types of fiction. Some great literary influences in her life include Edgar Allen Poe, Shakespeare, Francine Rivers and J K Rowling.

Her first love, besides her family, reading, and writing, is travel. She's backpacked through Europe, visited orphanages in China, and landed in a helicopter on a glacier in Alaska.

Ciara is extremely sociable and can be found at Facebook @ciaraknightwrites, Twitter @ciaratknight, Goodreads, Pinterest, and her website ciaraknight.com.

Made in the USA
Lexington, KY
28 January 2017